Sugar and Spice

Also by Lisa Papademetriou

CANDY APPLE BOOKS

Accidentally Fabulous

Accidentally Famous

Accidentally Fooled

Accidentally Friends

How to Be a Girly Girl in Just Ten Days

Ice Dreams

CONFECTIONATELY YOURS

Save the Cupcake!

Taking the Cake!

OTHER NOVELS

Chasing Normal

Drop

M or F?

Siren's Storm

Sixth-Grade Glommers, Norks, and Me

The Wizard, the Witch, and Two Girls from Jersey

Confectionately Yours

Sugar and Spice

Lisa Papademetriou

SCHOLASTIC INC.

If you purchased this book without a cover, you should be aware that this book is stolen property. It was reported as "unsold and destroyed" to the publisher, and neither the author nor the publisher has received any payment for this "stripped book."

No part of this publication may be reproduced, stored in a retrieval system, or transmitted in any form or by any means, electronic, mechanical, photocopying, recording, or otherwise, without written permission of the publisher. For information regarding permission, write to Scholastic Inc., Attention: Permissions Department, 557 Broadway, New York, NY 10012.

All activities in this book should be performed with adult supervision. The publisher and author disclaim all liability for any accidents or injuries or loss that may occur as a result of the use or misuse of the information and guidance given in this book.

ISBN 978-0-545-22230-3

Copyright © 2013 by Lisa Papademetriou
Recipes copyright © 2013 by Zoë Papademetriou

All rights reserved. Published by Scholastic Inc. SCHOLASTIC and associated logos are trademarks and/or registered trademarks of Scholastic Inc.

12 11 10 9 8 7 6 5 4 3 2 1   13 14 15 16 17 18/0

Printed in the U.S.A.   40

First printing, February 2013

Book design by Yaffa Jaskoll

To Amelia Chalfant

Down in Flames

"You know, this dance would be totally great," Marco says as he takes a cupcake from the platter I brought, "if it weren't so much like an execution."

"Tell me about it." The boys are lined up against one wall of the gym; the girls are lined up against the other. The refreshments table and decorations are the only clues that we're not here for a game of dodgeball. "The music here is better than at most executions, though."

"What flavor is this?" Marco asks, taking another bite of cupcake.

"Pistachio-rosewater."

"Weird, but good," he pronounces. Then he pulls a small

video camera from his pocket and trains it on the cupcake. "Pistachio-rosewater cupcakes by Hayley Hicks," he narrates, then swings the camera to face me. "How did you come up with this flavor, Hayley?"

I'm not sure how to answer this. I mean, I came up with it in my mind. "Through the power of pistachio nuts?"

"Hayley! C'mere!" In a corner, I see Meghan pointing with one hand and waving at me with the other. She's standing halfway underneath the bleachers.

"You'll be sorry," Marco says as he aims his video cam at Meghan.

"I usually am," I tell him, but I go over to join Meghan, anyway.

"Guess what this is!" Meghan says, pointing to a black metal box-like thing.

"Does it take dental X-rays?" I ask.

"It's a fog machine!" Meghan crows. She does a goofy little jig. She's wearing a pink dress with white polka dots and turquoise tights, and her bangs are a matching shade of pink. She looks like a crazy tropical bird doing a peculiar mating dance.

"You brought a fog machine to the Winter Dance?"

"Of course not!" Meghan huffs. "I took it out of the drama department's prop closet."

"But . . . why?"

"Nobody's dancing!"

"So?"

"So — I'm the seventh-grade class rep! I can't let the dance go down in flames."

"No, I mean, so what does the fog machine have to do with anything?"

"Look, everyone's too embarrassed to be the first one out on the floor. So I figure that if we pump a little haze into the gym . . ."

"People won't be able to see one another?"

"Right. And we'll get the dancing started! There's only one problem. I can't figure out how to turn this thing on." Meghan flips a switch. Then she flips it the other way. Nothing happens.

"Is it plugged in?"

"Yep."

"Let me see." I don't mean to brag, but I've got a gift for mechanical things. I'm the only person in our house who can work the old-fashioned alarm clock. Gran can barely even check voice mail. And the other day, when the industrial blender was on the fritz, I managed to get it going again. Meghan steps away from the fog machine, and I inspect it. The only switch seems to be the one she was fiddling with. I flip it, then wait. I flip it back. "Hmm . . ." I give the fog machine a kick.

Sure enough, fog starts to spew from the front nozzle.

"Brilliant!" Meghan cries.

I shrug. "That's what got the mixer going again."

A cloud shoots across the floor of the gym, and the crowd lining the walls lets out an "Ooo!"

The girls are the first to make a move. Leslie Fairstein has clearly been looking for an excuse to storm the dance floor. She grabs Farrah Akers's hand and drags her out into the middle of the gym. Soon, Omar Gomez and Jamil Singh are bopping around under a basketball hoop, and then a few eighth-grade girls I know from my bus head out. Once the eighth graders are out there, the sixthies feel free to stampede. The deejay takes the hint and turns up an Ashley Violetta song, and soon everyone is grooving.

"I'm a *genius*!" Meghan squeals as she watches the crowd.

The smoke has a strange, sickly sweet smell, and it's still pouring from the machine like Old Faithful.

"A demented genius," I agree. I see Marco over by the snack table, videotaping the dancing crowd. I wave; he grins and waves back. Another dance tune comes on, and Marco disappears in the rapidly advancing cloud of smog. "I think that's enough."

"Yeah, it's getting pretty smoky in here," Meghan agrees. She leans over and flips the switch.

Fog keeps on spewing.

Meghan flips the switch again. Off, on, off. I give the machine another kick. Twice as much fog starts coming out.

"Make it stop!" Meghan cries, then starts coughing.

"I can't!"

"What are you two doing?" demands a voice. Through the haze, I see that my ex–best friend, Artie, is glaring at us. Suddenly, I find myself hoping for more smoke, so that I can disappear entirely. "Where did you get a fog machine?"

"Meghan found it," I say, and then feel like a jerk.

"Did you get it from the drama department?" Artie demands.

Artie is a dramarama. From the look on her face, you'd think that her own house had been plundered. Like it's *her* fog machine.

"I borrowed it," Meghan says politely. "Um, do you know how to turn it off?"

At that moment, someone pulls a fire alarm.

"Oh, boy," Meghan says.

And then the sprinklers go off.

A few people shriek, and girls in dresses trot toward the exits while chaperones urge everyone to stay calm. Meghan, Artie, and I stand stock-still, watching the mayhem for a few moments. Fog is still pouring from the machine, by the way.

Suddenly, the sprinklers stop, and at almost the same moment the fog stops.

"Oh, whew!" I say. "It finally shut itself off."

"Ahem."

Meghan's face has gone white. She gestures for me to turn around, and when I do, I see the frowning face of Ms. Lang, the drama teacher. She's holding the power cord to the fog machine in her hand. Clearly, she just yanked it from the wall.

"Good thinking," Meghan tells her.

Ms. Lang cocks her head. "Yes," she says. "And do you know what is *not* good thinking? Taking drama department property without permission." She looks at Artie with a raised eyebrow. "I'm surprised to see you mixed up in this, Artemis."

"She wasn't —" I start, but Ms. Lang holds up her hand in a *Silence!* gesture. I mash my lips together.

Artie squirms, but she doesn't say anything.

"I'm giving you all a week of detention," Ms. Lang announces. "You can repair props and costumes to make up for the fact that you took the fog machine."

Meghan nods. "Well, I think that sounds fair —"

"I'm not really interested in your opinion, Ms. Markerson," Ms. Lang snaps.

"Okay," Meghan says.

The drama teacher shoots one last Look of Doom in Artie's direction. My Ex-Best sort of cringes, but she doesn't say anything.

"Artie," I tell her, "I'm so —"

But she's already stomping off.

Meghan sighs. "That didn't go too well."

I shrug. "Well . . . at least we got people to dance."

Meghan looks at me for a long moment. "You know, Hayley," she says, "I think maybe I'm a bad influence on you."

The smog is lifting in the gym. Okay, so we kind of made a mess of things. But the dance wasn't much fun until we did. In a way, I guess it's better to go down in flames and smoke than it is to just putter along until you fall off a cliff.

It occurs to me that I never would've thought that a year ago. Puttering along used to be what I was all about.

I guess maybe Meghan *is* a bad influence on me.

It's cold outside, and half the kids are running around like lunatics while the other half huddle up like penguins to keep one another warm. Everyone is talking and laughing, though, and I have to say that the dance seems like a pretty big success. I wish Meghan was here to see the happy crowd, but she has darted off to return the fog machine to the prop closet.

I hold on to the plate of cupcakes I grabbed on my way out the door. I wasn't sure if the teachers were going to send everyone home, or what, and I didn't want my treats to go to waste.

"Thanks, Hayley!" Jamil says as he grabs one of the cupcakes. He darts off. I offer a cupcake to Leslie, and soon Fatimah and Yolanda have each taken one, too. "Is the music still going?" Leslie asks. "I can hardly wait to get back out on the dance floor!" She hops from one foot to the other.

"All right, everyone!" Ms. Lang announces. She has a big drama voice, and people quiet down the minute she starts to speak. "You may return to the gym in a calm and orderly fashion! Calm and orderly — I am talking to you, Omar Gutierrez!"

Omar stops trying to smash a cupcake in Jamil's face and instead takes a calm, orderly bite.

The other chaperones, including Ms. Sweet, the earth science teacher, and Mr. Charles, the Latin teacher everyone hates, herd the kids back into the gym.

I hang back a little.

Personally, I like the cold. And my dress is velvet, with long sleeves, so I'm not completely freezing. A lot of the other girls are wearing halter tops or one-shoulder tanks with teeny minis, and I feel sorry for them as they totter on their high heels toward the gym.

I notice someone else hovering around at the edge of the crowd. "Hey, Kyle."

"Who is that?" He gives me a warm smile. His blond curls tumble down his forehead, almost hiding his eyes. "Fred?"

"You got it." Kyle calls me Fred sometimes. That's because the day I met him, I was wearing a shirt that said *Fred* on it. He couldn't see the name, of course, because he's legally blind. But I didn't know he was blind, so I just thought he couldn't read. I kept saying, "You can call me Fred," like *dur*. Then I realized the truth and I felt like a huge loser, but Kyle was really sweet about it.

"Want a cupcake?" I offer.

Kyle's eyes crinkle in amusement. "Do you just wander around with a plate of cupcakes all the time, Hayley?"

"I should. I'd be more popular."

"Why would you want to be more popular?" Kyle asks.

Interesting question. I'm not sure how to answer it. "Okay, well, I have cupcakes, anyway." I hand him one.

"Thanks," he says as he takes a bite. "This is awesome! I love pistachios. What's this?" He picks a flower off the top.

"A sugared violet."

Kyle nibbles a petal. "What color?"

"Blue."

"Faithfulness," he says, then pops the whole thing in his mouth.

"What?"

He holds up his finger and chews for a moment. Once he swallows, he says, "A long time ago, people used to send each other messages with flowers. In Victorian times. You could send a bouquet, and it would tell someone exactly how you felt about them. Violets meant faithfulness."

"What do roses mean?" I ask, thinking about the rosewater in the cupcake.

"Depends on the color — anything from love to sleep."

"You know a lot of weird stuff, Kyle."

"I pride myself on odd knowledge. I can't play sports, so . . ."

"What are you two still doing out here?" Marco asks as he comes up to us, camera in hand.

"We were just heading in," I say.

"We were?" Kyle smiles.

"In case you hadn't noticed, Kyle, it's freezing out here," I say.

"I *hadn't* really noticed," he says, and takes another bite of the cupcake.

There's an awkward little pause. I feel as if that sentence is a message, like a flower, but I'm not exactly sure what it means.

"Well, I'm going inside," Marco says at last. We all start toward the door. The last few kids are trickling in, and just my luck, it's Artie with her dramarama buddies, Chang and Kelley. Artie whispers something to Chang, who glares at me. Then they go through the door, and Artie deliberately lets it fall on my shoulder.

"What was *that*?" Marco asks, pulling the camera away from his face.

"Did you catch it?" I ask.

"Yeah."

"What did I miss?" Kyle asks.

"A look of disgust and assault with a door," Marco tells him.

"Artie's mad at me," I explain.

Kyle shrugs. "So, what else is new?"

Right. What else is new? Artie used to be my Best. Now she's my Worst.

And that's just the way it is.

There's no light coming from beneath my bedroom door when I get home, so I turn the knob carefully and give a gentle push. I don't want to wake my little sister, Chloe.

Back when we used to live in a house, Chloe and I each had our own room. But that was before our parents divorced, before Mom lost her job, before we moved in with Gran. Now we live above the Tea Room. It's been hard to get used to sharing my space . . . but it has been good, too. I like lying in the dark and chatting with Chloe until one of us falls asleep. And I know she likes it, too.

Chloe used to have an imaginary friend named Horatio. But he's disappeared. I like to think it's partly because of me. And maybe partly because of her new best friend, Rupert, who lives nearby.

On the other hand, sometimes I wish I could just burst into my room and flop on my bed. Maybe read for a while. Play music. Sometimes it's nice to be alone. You know, sometimes — like now.

I creep into the room so quietly that my heart nearly catapults out of my skin when Chloe says, "Hi, Hayley."

I look over at her bed, which is still made, and then I

realize that she's sitting on the window seat. The bay window frames her small body. She's wearing a long, pale pink sleep shirt with a cute kitten on it, and she looks very young to me, much younger than eight.

"Can't sleep?" I ask, kicking off my shoes.

Chloe turns back to the window and sighs. She has insomnia sometimes. It doesn't usually keep her up all night, but it's enough to disrupt her sleep and make her tired the next morning.

I sit down across from her. The shades are pulled up, and the lace curtains create a thin screen between our house and the night. We live on a fairly busy street, and light plays across her face as cars pass by. Chloe isn't looking at me. She's looking up, toward the sky.

Almost as if she can hear me wondering what she's thinking about, she says, "Everyone sees the same moon."

I look up at it — an uneven, lopsided moon tonight. The dark shadows scar its white face, but it's still beautiful. I imagine our dad, who's away on a business trip, looking up at the lumpy moon and missing us as much as Chloe is missing him right now. I take her hand. "It's shining on everyone," I tell Chloe.

"Unless it's cloudy."

"Right. But it's still there, anyway."

Chloe looks at me, her face serious. "Just because someone moves away, it doesn't mean they're gone forever."

There's a note of pain in her voice that stabs at my heart.
We see our dad pretty regularly even though he and our
mom are divorced, but I hadn't realized that she missed him
so much. "It doesn't mean that," I tell her. "Not at all."

"Okay."

"Dad's probably missing us even more than we're missing him," I say. "He loves us. You know that, right? He totally
loves you."

Chloe's eyebrows draw together. She seems to think
about this for a few moments. "Okay," she says again.

There doesn't seem to be any reason to rush to bed. My
mind is spinning, and I'm sure Chloe's still is, too, and right
now, I'm really glad we share this room, so that we can be
here together. So we just stay on the window seat for a while,
looking out at the busy restaurants and dark art galleries,
and up at the sky.

Sometimes, insomnia's not so bad.

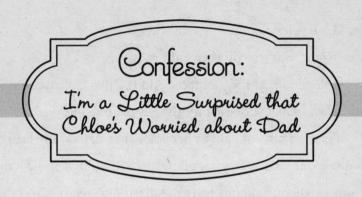

Confession:
I'm a Little Surprised that Chloe's Worried about Dad

It has been over a year since our father moved out. It has been six months since we moved out of our old house and in with Gran. And this is the first time Chloe has seemed worried that Dad might forget us.

It's a little odd. After all, Dad introduced us to his new girlfriend, Annie, in the fall. I wasn't that impressed, but Chloe liked Annie right away — a lot, which was lucky for Annie. For a while there, it was a little like Anniepalooza. We never saw Dad without her. We even had to spend Thanksgiving with Annie and her parents at a restaurant, which turned into a hideous spectacle when I barfed paella into the bread basket, but that's another story.

But lately, Dad has been spending more time with just us. We still hang with Annie once in a while, but we've managed to have Dad all to ourselves for movie nights, bowling, and a concert.

And even the time we do spend with Annie has been more fun. She took us out for Thai food. She held a long conversation in Thai with the waiter, and when he returned, he heaped our table with all sorts of delicious-smelling things that I'd never heard of. It was one of the best meals I've ever had. We also all went to laser tag together, and it turns out that Annie has a crazy competitive streak and killer aim. She was taking down everyone — she had no problem blasting at an entire birthday party full of nine-year-old boys — which made it *way* fun. At the end, Chloe was laughing so hard that I was worried she might pass out.

So, why would Chloe be worried about Dad?

Maybe she wonders whether Dad and Annie might get married. Maybe she's worried about what that could mean . . . like, would they want to have kids? Would Dad start a whole new family and forget about us? Would we just be these little add-ons, the kids that show up every

other weekend, while the other kids are Dad's "perma-
nent kids"?

Wait.

Now *I'm* worried.

Great.

I guess Chloe has good reasons to freak out.

Baklava Cupcakes

(makes approximately 12 cupcakes)

When the weather gets cold, I love flavors like cinnamon and allspice. They make you feel warm from the inside out.

INGREDIENTS FOR NUT MIX:
- 1/2 cup pistachio nuts
- 1/2 cup walnuts
- 1/2 cup almonds
- 1/4 cup granulated sugar

INGREDIENTS FOR SYRUP:
- 1/4 cup granulated sugar
- 1/2 cup honey
- 1/2 cup water
- A pinch of whole cloves (3–4 pieces)
- 1/8 teaspoon allspice
- 1/8 teaspoon ground cinnamon

INGREDIENTS FOR CUPCAKES:

   1/2 cup milk

   1/2 cup yogurt

   1/3 cup canola oil

   3/4 cup granulated sugar

   1/2 teaspoon almond extract

   1 teaspoon vanilla extract

   1-1/4 cups all-purpose flour

   3/4 teaspoon baking powder

   1/2 teaspoon baking soda

   1/2 teaspoon ground cinnamon

   1/4 teaspoon allspice

   1/8 teaspoon ground cloves

   1/2 teaspoon salt

INSTRUCTIONS:

1. Preheat the oven to 350°F. Line a muffin pan with aluminum cupcake liners, NOT paper ones. (Trust me!)

2. To prepare the nut mix, place the nuts on a baking sheet and lightly toast them in the oven, approximately 15 minutes. Remove

and allow them to cool before stirring them together with the sugar and chopping them up. Divide the nut mix equally among the cupcake liners.

3. In a small saucepan, combine all of the syrup ingredients and heat on medium, stirring until the sugar is completely dissolved. Turn off the heat and set aside.

4. In a large bowl, whisk together the milk, yogurt, oil, sugar, almond extract, and vanilla extract, and set aside.

5. In a separate bowl, sift together the flour, baking powder, baking soda, cinnamon, allspice, cloves, and salt, and mix.

6. Add the dry ingredients to the wet ones a little bit at a time, and combine using a whisk or handheld mixer, stopping to scrape the sides of the bowl a few times, until no lumps remain.

7. Fill the cupcake liners two-thirds of the way with batter, pouring it right onto the nut mix, and bake for 22–24 minutes, until an inserted toothpick comes out clean. Use the toothpick

to poke several holes into the tops of each cupcake. Rewarm the syrup in the saucepan and then remove it from stove; discard the whole cloves. Then spoon equal amounts on top of each cupcake while they're still warm, allowing the syrup to soak into the cupcake before serving. Frosting, or a sprinkle of confectioners' sugar, on top is optional, but should be added after the cupcakes have completely cooled.

The Language of Cupcakes

I peer through the little window on the oven and see that the domes of my cupcakes have turned golden brown. This is a trial batch. I'm testing a new flavor, code-named: Reassurance.

The sweet smell of cinnamon and vanilla wafts through the café as I pull the hot baking tin from the oven. I sneak a peek at the table by the window, where Chloe and Rupert are busy reading together. She doesn't look up from her novel, and I wonder if the scent of the cupcakes has reached her yet. I wonder if the smell alone is enough to ease her mind.

I figure that if the Victorians can have a language of flowers, I can have my own language of cupcakes. The first message is for my sister.

The bell over the door jingles and a cheery-faced Mr. Malik steps in. "Where is she?" he demands.

"Who?"

"My grandmother! Where is she? I can smell the aroma of her famous Victoria sponge cake." His dark eyes twinkle, and his face creases from his eyes to his chin. Mr. Malik must be seventy years old. He owns the flower shop next door, and he's my gran's good friend. "It smells like my childhood in here, like sitting on Grandmummy's lap at teatime."

"I'm just making cupcakes."

"Well, I must have one immediately!"

"I haven't frosted them yet."

"Even better. Frosting is an abomination."

I lift one of the cupcakes from the tin, careful not to burn my fingertips. I place it on a plate and pass it to Mr. Malik. "No charge."

"You'll never make money that way." He tries and utterly fails to look disapproving.

"It's a test batch."

Mr. Malik takes a bite and smiles. "You have passed the

test, my dear Hayley. Your granddaughter has created another masterpiece, Mrs. Wilson," he says to Gran, who has just appeared behind the counter.

"I can't say that I'm surprised, Mr. Malik," she replies. "Ah, it smells like Easter morning in here."

Gran is British and Mr. Malik is Pakistani, and they're a little formal with each other, even though they've been good friends for years.

"May I have one?" Chloe appears at the counter and eyes the cupcakes. I smile at her, glad that the warm smell has drawn her over.

"Only one?" Gran asks. "Wouldn't Rupert like one?"

Chloe blushes. "I don't want to take too many. I thought we could share."

"I made them for you," I say.

Chloe beams as I hand over two plates. "Thanks!" She starts to turn away but pauses. "I love you," she says, and then moves to join her friend.

"How lovely," Mr. Malik says.

"These girls are wonderful together," Gran agrees.

I feel warm all over. My language of cupcakes works!

The door bangs open and a cold breeze blows across the café. A large figure wrapped in a black shawl blocks the winter light. My warm, fuzzy feeling disappears.

"Hello, Ms. Malik," Gran says. "To what do we owe this unexpected pleasure?"

Mr. Malik's sister glowers at my grandmother as she steps inside the warm café. Uzma and Gran have kind of been in a fight for years. Here's what happened: I picked a dead leaf off a plant in Mr. Malik's flower shop. Uzma yelled at me. Gran defended me. Uzma called her an imperialist. Gran stormed out. Mr. Malik came by later with apology flowers. The end.

That was five years ago, and Uzma is still scowling. She ignores Gran. "Mamoo is being perfectly unreasonable," she says to Mr. Malik. "Now he's refusing to speak to Rana at all, and she can't get him to apologize to Mrs. Azbahi!"

Mr. Malik thinks this over. "So?"

"So? So? Our uncle has offended a dear family friend, and he won't even listen to his own daughter!" Uzma looks outraged.

"Mamoo has always been unreasonable."

"But — but —" Uzma's face has turned red. She looks like she might explode. "You should phone him!"

"My dear sister, I am not getting involved in this affair, and I suggest that you don't, either. You know Mamoo. He'll apologize to Mrs. Azbahi when he is ready, and not before."

Uzma sputters. She gapes at me, as if she thinks I might stand up for her. I have no idea what to say, so I just shrug. "Cupcake?" I ask.

She lets out something that sounds like a growl and turns to blast out of the café.

Gran looks at Mr. Malik. "What a pleasant visit," she says.

He sighs. "My sister is a brilliant woman, but she's restless. Our extended family is in Pakistan, and her dearest friends have families of their own. . . . She needs something to occupy her attention. Otherwise she'll drive herself — and everyone else — crazy."

Gran purses her lips and looks out the window, toward the empty space where Uzma Malik blew past in a tornado of black fabric. "Perhaps I should get to know your sister," she says thoughtfully.

"She really is a wonderful person," Mr. Malik says. He brushes cupcake crumbs from his fingertips and bows toward me. "Thank you for the delicious treat, and the delightful company. Mrs. Wilson, I will return on Thursday with your flowers."

"I look forward to it, Mr. Malik," Gran replies.

"Me, too," I put in.

Mr. Malik's eyes crinkle in a smile. It's so amazing to think that he and Uzma have the same blood, the same parents, and a shared history. How can two people have so much in common, and yet be so completely different?

I look over at Chloe, happily reading with quiet Rupert by the window.

I guess people could ask the same thing about us.

"The members of the girls' lacrosse team will be dismissed early today, at 1:30. Auditions for the Crazy Flapper Improv Group will be held Wednesday during lunch, in the auditorium. This is a reminder that anyone found chewing gum . . ."

I doodle a cupcake on the cover of my notebook and stare at the clock. It's homeroom, and there are five more minutes of announcements to go.

Marco trains his video camera on the cover of my notebook. "As you can see," he narrates quietly as he leans over from the desk beside mine, "Hayley thinks about cupcakes even during off-hours."

I draw a cross-eyed goofy face, and he zooms in on it.

A folded paper triangle pings my toe. Subtly, I lean over and pick it up, then smooth it out against my notebook. It's from the desk on the other side of mine: Meghan's.

What's with the evil look that Artie is giving you?

I glance over at Artie, who looks like she's trying to bore a hole in my skull with her eyes. Meghan leans toward me and waves at Artie. Then she gives her a little *Call me* sign. I stifle a giggle, but Artie looks like she's about to scream. She looks away, at her new dramarama buddy Chang Xiao. But Chang is chatting with Kelley. Artie laughs along with something they say, but neither one of them seems to notice her.

I watch my Ex-Best as she opens a book and starts to read.

Wow. That's weird. I guess making Ms. Lang mad comes with a cost.

I look over at Meghan, who lifts an eyebrow. She's noticed the same weirdness I have. She rolls her eyes. Translation: Detention is gonna be *fun*.

". . . and anyone interested in volunteering —"

There's a brief scuffling sound, then a whine of feedback on the PA system. I hear some muffled banging, like someone is trying to get in a door at the other end of the school. I glance over at Meghan, whose eyes are wide.

"Yo, Adams Middle School! It's Omar —"

"— and Jamil!"

"— and we're keepin' it real! Yo, here's a little rap for all my sisters and brothers —"

"— and even the others —"

"— hope you're dealin' with the feelin' that this school's kinda whack —"

"— and your teachers are freakin' like they're 'bout to attack —"

"— well, don't let it get ugly and don't let life get hairy —"

"— just try to keep your cool like Ben and Jerry!"

"Peace out, yo!"

At that moment, the bell rings, and our class erupts. Everyone's talking and laughing, and nobody is paying attention to Ms. Anderson, who keeps shouting, "Passing period is supposed to be quiet, people! Quiet!"

Marco swings his video camera around, capturing the mayhem. ·

"Did you get the whole rap on video?" I ask him.

He nods. "Lucky I didn't shut if off before they started. What *was* that?"

"A rap bomb," Meghan explains. "They just busted in and took over the announcements."

"Aren't they going to get into trouble?" I ask.

Meghan laughs. "Oh, yeah." Then she looks at Marco. "Please delete that laugh from your video."

Marco turns it off. "Done."

"Worried Omar and Jamil might get mad?" I ask.

"I just don't want them to rap bomb my next oral report," Meghan says.

"Better safe than sorry," Marco agrees. He stuffs the video camera into his backpack.

I have no clue what he's going to do with all of the stuff he's taping.

Confession:
Marco Takes the Best Photos

I have a framed photo of me and Artie on my bedside table. It's from last year. We were at the park, and you can see that the leaves on the trees behind us are turning red and orange. Artie has her arm around my neck, and I'm laughing. Artie is looking straight at the camera with this little smile on her face, like she's feeling kind of smug because she just said something hilarious. My mouth is wide open, and you can only see half of my face. It's not the most flattering shot, but I love that photo.

I love it so much that I haven't taken it down, even though I don't really love Artie anymore.

There's something about it — it really captures how I

was feeling at that moment. I was just . . . happy. It wasn't complicated. Being with Artie was easy. The park was beautiful. The word I think of when I see that photo is *radiant*.

Marco took the photo.

He's always been into photography. Even when we were little kids, he would wander around with an old digital camera, snapping photos of everyone on the playground. I remember in fifth grade, Marco found out about this photography camp. He was dying to go. It was run by a local photographer, and he would've learned all about composition and lighting, and he even would've gotten to develop his own film in a darkroom, old-school style. He was so excited; he talked about it for a week before he got up the nerve to ask his parents about it.

But when he did, Marco's dad told him that he'd already signed him up for soccer camp. Soccer players can get college scholarships, his dad had said. Photography is a waste of time, he'd said. Forget about it, he'd said.

Well, Marco never mentioned the photography camp again . . . but I'm not sure he ever forgot about it.

It's weird how things work out. Like, now Marco's been kicked off the soccer team . . . but he's picked up a video camera. So that might end up being a cool thing. He's good with pictures, that's all I know.

I can't wait to see what he does with it.

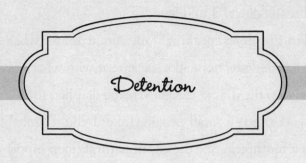

Detention

*M*eghan dashes through the door to the costume shop, her pink bangs plastered to her forehead.

Ms. Lang flares her nostrils and purses her lips into a frown. "You're late."

"I know." Meghan gulps some air and perches on a stool. "Someone had a question about the elections for class rep next year, and so I started explaining —"

I make a cutting motion across my throat. Ms. Lang is not in a good mood. The first thing she said to me when I walked through the door was, "I guess you think it's pretty hilarious to take an expensive item from the drama department and use it for your own amusement, don't you?"

"I really don't," I told her.

"I'm not done speaking!" she shouted, and when Artie made a little *hmm* noise like she agreed with what Ms. Lang was saying, the drama teacher screamed at her, too.

Ms. Lang is a small person. Like, I could probably use her as a toothpick. She dresses in natural fiber, hippie-chick clothes and has these orange rectangular glasses. She wears her hair in a French twist, and she might even be pretty . . . if she weren't so scary.

As Meghan continues to babble away, I notice Ms. Lang's eyebrows creeping up so far that they're threatening to become part of her scalp. I intensify my *Cut* motion and shake my head.

Meghan finally clues in. "And that's why I can stop talking now," she says. "Sorry."

Ms. Lang narrows her eyes like a dangerous iguana. Then she sucks in a breath. "I'm not here to babysit you three. What I want you to do is to sort through the costumes. Separate anything that is torn or soiled so that it can be repaired. I want everything in top shape for the Spring Spectacular."

"That sounds fun!" Meghan says, and Ms. Lang gives her a look that could vaporize her.

"It's not meant to be fun," Ms. Lang says. "When you've completed that task, you can get busy cleaning the floors and organizing the small props. I'll be back to check on your progress in half an hour." And she swoops out the door.

Meghan stares at the empty door frame for a moment. "Okay, well, that's cool," she says.

"Could you please just stop talking for thirty seconds?" Artie snaps. "You drive everyone nuts!"

Meghan folds her arms across her chest, and I can tell that something unpleasant is about to happen, so I jump in with, "Hey, why don't I start on this rack of guy stuff, Artie, and maybe you can do gowns? Meg, why don't you take a look at accessories?"

Meghan looks at me, then back at Artie, like she's considering whether it's worth her while to say something nasty. I guess it isn't, because she says, "Okay, Hayley. Good plan."

Artie huffs out a sigh. "Fine," she says. "Everything from the fall musical is messed up, so I'll start with those things." She makes her way over to a rack of clothes.

The costume shop is small and narrow, a long room in the basement of the building. It's got two doors and is crammed with clothes, boxes, props, hats, shoes, scarves, and a million other accessories. Every surface is crammed with stuff. There's a musty, old-clothes smell, but I don't mind it. It's messy but cozy, almost nest-like, down here.

I start by looking over suit jackets. Most of these seem to be in good shape. I notice a pinstripe with a frayed cuff, and place it aside. Cream linen with an ink stain — to the side. Then there are a few things that just need to be cleaned. I make space for them and put them in a neat little section. This kind of work calls out to my inner organizer, and after a while, I find I'm actually enjoying it.

"Hmm," Meghan says from across the room. When I look over, I see she's wearing a pair of severe glasses and has draped herself in a poncho. "I suppose you think it's amusing to organize the clothes for our Spring Spectacular?" she asks, pursing her lips into a frown. She looks freakishly like Ms. Lang.

"Cut it out," Artie tells her.

Meghan grumbles. "If I want your opinion, Artemis Steele, believe me, I'll ask for it."

I can't help giggling, and Artie shoots me a glare.

"Oh, good work, Artemis," Meghan says in her best Ms. Lang voice. "Excellent Stare of Doom!"

Before Artie can reply, I grab a sparkly headband and pop it onto my hair. "Um, hey, Ms. Lang — I have a great idea! Is it okay if the seventh-grade class council borrows the drama department van so we can go out for ice cream? Hayley can work the brakes while I turn the steering wheel!" Then I give a crazy, goofy smile that's *very* Meghan.

Meghan laughs.

"Would you guys knock it off?" Artie says. "We're supposed to be organizing this stuff, not hosting a talent show."

Meghan's eyes light up in a way I know well. Too well. It's that terrifying *I have an idea* look that she gets sometimes.

Ms. Lang chooses that moment to check on us. She stops in the doorway and looks Meghan up and down. "Why are you wearing a poncho?" she asks.

"Just . . . uh . . . checking the size." Meghan bites her lip and pulls it off over her head.

Ms. Lang looks at me, and I feel my blood curdle like old milk. I yank the headband off my head.

"You girls are supposed to be organizing, not joking around," Ms. Lang says.

"That's what I said," Artie puts in.

"If I want your opinion, Artemis, I'll ask for it," Ms. Lang says, and she sounds so much like Meghan did a minute ago that I have to pretend to sneeze in order to hide my giggle. Ms. Lang turns to me. "You and Ms. Markerson may move on to scrubbing the floor," she says. "The cleaning supplies are in the closet. And if I hear any more noise coming from this room, believe me, I can find work for all three of you for next week, too."

She stomps off, like a teeny tiny Godzilla.

Artie doesn't actually say "I told you," but she makes a little three-pitch hum, like *hmm-HMM-hmm*, that sounds exactly the same. I can read her mind, anyway, and I know that's what she's thinking.

Meghan sighs and pulls off her fake glasses.

"Come on," I say, and we go get the bucket and rags from the closet. Meghan fills the bucket while I move furniture from the far corner.

"So, okay, here's the idea," Meghan whispers as she dips a rag into the soapy water.

"No."

"You don't even know what it is!"

"Shh!" This is from Artie.

Meghan rolls her eyes at Artie, then turns back to me. "Hayley — it's awesome! We'll hold a talent show!"

"Why?"

"Why? Because people at this school have talent, that's why!" Meghan insists. "Like Ava, with her capoeira. And Elmo Jackson's crazy puppets — have you seen them? And Julian Descartes — he can do, like, five hula hoops at a time! Oh, and Maria Chatzopolous's juggling act! Seriously, why should the dramaramas be the only ones who appear onstage at Adams Middle?"

I sigh. Here is the problem with Meghan's ideas: They *do* sound fun. That's where all the trouble starts.

I scrub some disgusting brown crust from a baseboard. "But . . . we'd have to use the stage. Which means we'd have to get Ms. Lang to say yes."

"That's true. . . ."

Meghan and I peek over at Artie, who doesn't look up from the gowns she's sorting. "Forget it," she says. "There's no way I'm helping you two."

Meghan shrugs and smiles at me. It's a conspiratorial smile, like she thinks Artie will come around. But I shake my head.

I've known Artie for years. I know how stubborn she can be.

When she says no way, she means it.

"How was your prison term?" Gran asks as she hands me a dripping plate. "Were you forced into hard labor?"

"Kind of. We had to clean out the costume department." I wipe the plate with a towel and place it in the cabinet. Yes, we have a dishwasher, but Gran hardly ever uses it. She hates to waste water, she says, and goes old-school with a bucket of soapy water in the sink and then a quick rinse. But I know the truth — Gran just loves washing dishes. You can tell by the way she hums old show tunes while she does it.

I don't mind it, either. Especially since it was just the two of us for dinner tonight. Mom is out on a date with Police Officer Ramon, and Chloe is over at Rupert's house. It's not like there's a huge stack of plates to deal with.

"Hah! Your mother will be glad to hear that you spent the day sorting. She'll probably want you to clean out your closet, now that you have so much experience."

"You mean she'll want me to clean out *her* closet. It's a disaster in there — someone should do an intervention."

"I wouldn't interfere with that, my dear, or you just may find yourself buried under twenty years' worth of old coats."

She has a point. Mom has never been good at getting rid of stuff. Even when we moved, she just packed it all into these huge stand-up wardrobe boxes. She said she couldn't deal with getting rid of everything. It's funny, because Mom is really organized . . . just not about clothes.

There's a rattle in the lock, and a moment later, Mom comes through the door followed by Ramon. Her cheeks are flushed pink from the cold, and her dark curls are wild beneath her red watch cap. "Hayley!" She beams. "How was dinner?"

"Great," I told her. "Gran made fish."

"Not shellfish, I hope," Ramon says with a wincing smile.

"No, my dear, I *do* try to avoid poisoning my granddaughter." Gran gives him a wink and hands me the last platter.

"Ah, I'll never live that day down!" Ramon jokes. "I still feel so awful about that, Hayley," he apologizes, sticking his hands deep into his coat pockets.

This past Thanksgiving, we had two celebrations. First, Ramon came over and brought paella, which had lobster in it. I gobbled it up . . . not knowing that I'm allergic to lobster. A few hours later, it was Barf City meets Hivetown in full view of a country club full of elegant rich people. Luckily, we were with my dad, Annie, and her parents, and her mom is a doctor. She took me back to her office for a shot.

"That was, like, *months* ago," I tell him. "Seriously, you don't have to apologize every time you see me. It's not like you did it on purpose."

"Or *did* he?" Gran says with a playful cackle.

"Maybe you should find out if my mother is allergic to anything," Mom suggests to Ramon, who laughs.

"Would you like tea?" Gran asks. "You two must be cold. I'll just put a pot on."

"I'd love some," Mom says, and Gran fills the kettle.

Ramon shakes his head. "I've got to get going."

"Well — thanks for a lovely evening." Mom smiles up at Ramon. He takes a step forward, like he's about to hug her, but she sticks out a hand for a shake. Then she sees her mistake and tries to give him a hug, but he's already got *his* hand out, so they end up doing this awkward little handshake-slap-on-the-back thing.

"Okay," Mom says brightly, and lets Ramon out the door.

"I'll call tomorrow?" he asks.

"Sounds good." Mom closes the door and covers her face in her hands. Then she giggles, and when she takes her fingers from her cheeks, they're pink again. "Oh, I'm so bad at this!"

Gran looks at me and smiles. I have to admit that Mom's pretty cute.

"He thinks you're adorable, darling," Gran says. "And you are." The kettle whistles and Gran pours boiling water over the tea. "I'll just let this steep for a few moments while I gather my laundry together."

"I've got some things in the dryer," Mom calls after her.

"I'll take care of it!"

With a sigh, Mom pulls off her cap and her coat and hangs them on the peg by the door. Then she kicks off her heavy boots and pads over to me in thick wool socks. "How was your day, sweetie?" she asks as she gives me a hug.

"Hmm . . . B plus, I guess. It was pretty good, except for detention."

"Oh, Hayley." Mom shakes her head.

"I know, I know. . . ." Mom isn't happy that I got detention, but she thinks Ms. Lang overreacted a little, so at least I'm not in trouble at home. "I never thought I'd be the kind of person who gets detention."

"You never got into trouble before you met Meghan," Mom points out. She sits down at the kitchen table.

"I know, but it's weird — Meghan is a straight-A student and class rep. She's just the only nerd I know who gets into trouble."

"Well . . . it's not as if your grades are suffering," Mom says thoughtfully.

I carefully carry her teacup over to the table. "So . . . how was your *date*?" I waggle my eyebrows.

Mom laughs. "Oh, Hayley, it's so strange to have my own daughter ask me that."

"Yeah. It's kind of strange to be your daughter and ask you."

We look at each other for a moment. I get the feeling that we both have more to say . . . but maybe neither one of us knows exactly what. Mom looks down at her teacup. Then she picks it up and takes a sip. "It's bizarre to be dating again. I kind of hate it."

"Really? But Ramon is so nice. . . ."

"He's very nice. But still — when you're out on a date . . ." Mom shrugs. "I always feel like I'm auditioning for something. Like, I had to sit there and chat about my day and the café and everything . . . but really, I just wanted to get home and have tea and find out how you and Chloe were doing."

"We're fine."

Mom presses her lips together, then takes another sip of tea. "Does Chloe seem . . . sad to you?"

"Yeah. I think maybe she's missing Dad."

Mom tilts her head, like she's considering it. The kitchen is quiet. The clock tick-tick-ticks on the wall and I hear the water running in the washing machine down the hall. It's nice to be here, alone with my mother. We don't actually spend much time together, just the two of us. And I'm relieved that she's noticed Chloe's mood, too. It's always good to know your parents are paying attention. It's comforting. "I guess we'll see," Mom says at last.

"She'll tell us sooner or later."

"Hmm." Mom looks at me from the corner of her eye, then nods. But I know what she's thinking: I hope it's sooner.

I'm thinking the exact same thing.

Confession:
Chloe Waits

*L*ast year, I caught Chloe crying alone in her room one afternoon. I asked her what was wrong, but she wouldn't tell me. She wouldn't even admit that anything *was* wrong.

For three weeks after that, she seemed sad.

I remember the date that I knew for sure that something was wrong. March 11. "Hey — what's Mara doing for her birthday this year?" I asked, checking the calendar. Chloe and Mara had been best friends since preschool.

"Nothing special," Chloe said.

Nothing special? That was not Mara's style. It wasn't Mara's mom's style, either. These were the people who had taken over the local beauty salon and given fourteen six-year-olds "Rock-star Makeovers" the year before.

I was sure that Mara was doing something for her birthday . . . and Chloe wasn't invited.

I fretted about it for another month but didn't hear a word. Finally, Chloe's teacher called Mom in for a conference. It turned out that Mara and two other girls had been picking on Chloe for months.

I don't know why Chloe hadn't told us. Maybe she didn't want to talk about it. Maybe she thought things would change. Maybe she was afraid Mom would do something big . . . which Mom, of course, did. She waited for the school year to be over (only another six weeks by then) and enrolled Chloe in a different school.

And that's when Chloe found Rupert. Her new best friend. Her *real* best friend.

I wonder how much sooner that could have happened if Chloe had just spoken up.

Raspberry Cupcakes

(makes approximately 12 cupcakes)

I top these with white-chocolate mint frosting. You could also just go with vanilla frosting . . . but why be normal?

INGREDIENTS:
- 1 cup milk
- 1 teaspoon apple cider vinegar
- 1-1/4 cups all-purpose flour
- 1 teaspoon baking powder
- 3/4 teaspoon baking soda
- 1/2 teaspoon salt
- 3/4 cup granulated sugar
- 1/3 cup canola oil
- 1 teaspoon vanilla extract
- 1 6-ounce container fresh raspberries (or equal amount frozen raspberries, thawed), mashed into pulp

INSTRUCTIONS:

1. Preheat the oven to 350°F. Line a muffin pan with cupcake liners.

2. In a large bowl, whisk together the milk and vinegar, and set aside for a few minutes to curdle.

3. In a separate bowl, sift together the flour, baking powder, baking soda, and salt.

4. Once the milk has curdled, add in the sugar, oil, vanilla extract, and raspberry pulp, and stir. Then slowly add the dry ingredients to the wet ones a little bit at a time, and combine using a whisk or handheld mixer, stopping to scrape the sides of the bowl a few times, until no lumps remain.

5. Fill cupcake liners two-thirds of the way and bake for 20–22 minutes. Transfer to a cooling rack, and let cool completely before frosting.

White-Chocolate Mint Frosting

INGREDIENTS:

4-1/2 ounces white chocolate, finely chopped

6 tablespoons margarine or butter

2 cups confectioners' sugar

1/2 teaspoon vanilla extract

1 teaspoon mint extract or minced fresh mint leaves (NOT peppermint)

Up to 1/4 cup milk

INSTRUCTIONS:

1. In a double boiler, melt the white chocolate until smooth, then remove and cool to room temperature. If you prefer, you can instead melt the white chocolate in a small bowl in the microwave, heating it on high for a few seconds at a time, then stirring until smooth. (Repeat heating if necessary, but don't overdo it!)

2. In a large bowl, with an electric mixer, cream the margarine or butter until it's a lighter color, about 2–3 minutes.

3. Slowly beat in the confectioners' sugar in 1/2-cup batches, adding the vanilla extract and either mint extract or minced fresh mint leaves about halfway through.

4. Add the melted white chocolate to the frosting and combine thoroughly. If the frosting seems too stiff and thick, add a little milk until the right consistency is reached. Continue mixing on high speed for about 3–7 minutes, until the frosting is light and fluffy. Place in the refrigerator until firm enough to frost, about 30 minutes.

Slices

"Daddy!" Chloe runs toward our father, who is waiting for us outside Sunrise Pizza.

"Hey!" He scoops her up and swings her around, and she squeals happily. "I'm so glad to see my girls!" Dad holds out his arm for a hug, and I step into it.

"We missed you," I say. *He still smells the same*, I think as I breathe in the scent of his clean, pressed shirt. He hasn't been gone long — we only missed one of our usual weekend dates, which is why we're seeing him on a school night — but, somehow, it seems like forever.

We head into the restaurant and take our favorite booth near the front. Chloe is bubbling over with excitement, telling Dad all about this science fair project that she's working on, which sort of gets me out of having to tell him about my second day of detention. She wants to know if different kinds of bread grow different kinds of mold, which seems kind of disgusting to me, but Dad is all into it and starts explaining how bread mold is the origin of penicillin. Then the waitress comes to take our order, and we get the usual — large pizza: half cheese, half pineapple and ham. I take a dollar instead of a Coke (Dad's standard deal, meant to encourage us to save money), but Chloe decides to get cranberry juice.

Then Dad holds up a small purple shopping bag. "I brought you guys a couple of things from Chicago," he says.

"How was your trip?" Chloe asks, her eyes glowing. "I've never been to Chicago!"

"Well, I hardly saw any of it," Dad admits. "I was mostly just in an office building and a hotel. But I got you these. . . ." He pulls out something wrapped in white tissue paper and hands it to me. When I unwrap it, I see long sticks, each topped with a paper office building. "It's the Willis Tower," Dad explains. "They're cupcake toppers."

"I love them!" I lean across the table and give him a peck on the cheek. "They're perfect! Where did you find them?"

"Oh, there was a specialty baking shop across the street from the office," Dad says. "I thought they might have something good, so I managed to dash in."

I'm really touched that my father took the time to go to a baking store to look for a gift for me while he was working. Dad isn't really a gift guy, usually. This is one way that Annie has been a good influence on him.

"And for you . . ." Dad pulls out a book and gives it to Chloe. It's *Chicago Poems*, by Carl Sandburg. "I don't know if you'll be interested, but I thought maybe you and Rupert might like to read a few. . . ."

Chloe touches the title, running her fingers over the letters. Her lip trembles a little, and tears spring into her eyes.

"Are you okay?" I ask, and that does it: Chloe starts crying for real — heaving, messy sobs. She leans against me, and I put my arm around her, and just then our pizza arrives, and we all have to sit there in awkward silence while Chloe cries and our waitress pretends not to see as she sets the pizza on a rack and puts plates in front of us.

Once the waitress darts away, Dad leans across the table. "Chloe, honey, I didn't mean to upset you. . . ." He flashes me a *Please help!* look.

"What's wrong, Chlo?" I ask.

"Nothing," she whimpers.

"That's so obviously a lie," I tell her, stroking her hair. "I mean, you're getting tears and snot all over my shirt."

Chloe takes a deep, shuddering breath. "Rupert's moving away!" she wails.

"What? How can he move away?" I ask, and realize that I'm wailing, too. Dad looks at me and shakes his head, like, *Not helpful.* I clear my throat. "Where's he moving?" I ask in what I hope is a much calmer tone.

Chloe takes a few deep breaths, and Dad serves up a slice of pineapple pizza for her. I help myself to cheese. Chloe takes a bite and chews slowly. "Rupert's father is getting out of his treatment facility," Chloe says. "He won't be living with his foster family anymore."

"Oh," I say. I hadn't even realized that Rupert *was* living with a foster family.

"He has to move across town," Chloe says. "He has to change schools."

"How does Rupert feel about all of this?" Dad asks.

"He says he misses his dad," Chloe admits. "But he also says that now he'll miss me." Her eyes sparkle, and a fat teardrop falls from her lower lashes to her cheek. "And I'll miss him."

"Oh, Chloe," I say, pulling her in for another hug. I don't know what to say — I really don't. Have you ever heard the term *soul mate*? Well, Rupert is like Chloe's little soul mate. They're like two peas.

"Look, Chloe, it's great that Rupert's father is ready to take care of him again," Dad says. "And it's good news that he isn't moving too far away. You know, Northampton has something called school choice — that means that you don't have to go to the school in your neighborhood. You can choose to go to a school across town."

"So, he may not have to change schools?" Chloe asks.

"Right. I don't know the situation. I'm just saying that it may not be as bad as you think."

Chloe takes another bite of pizza and chews thought-fully. "It still won't be the same, though."

Dad nods. He smiles, but he looks a little sad. "Nothing's ever the same, honey," he says. "Everything changes."

We all eat and think about that for a while. I'm a little surprised that Dad has managed to come through with words of wisdom . . . surprised, and happy. Usually Mom is the person we talk to about stuff like this.

"So, listen," I say finally. "I've got these new cupcake toppers. I think I'll make us some dessert when we get home."

"Chocolate cupcakes?" Chloe asks.

"Anything you want," I tell her, but secretly, I think chocolate would be perfect. I want to make something that says *comfort*. And what could be more comforting than that?

Late Again

"**G**ood news," Meghan says the minute I walk up to my locker.

"Anders's English test is canceled?" I guess.

"Antoine Kennedy is doing a karate demonstration for the talent show."

"We're having a talent show?"

Meghan's blue eyes go wide. "Don't you remember?" she asks.

"I didn't realize it was a definite thing," I tell her. "Have you cleared it with anyone?"

Meghan lets out a *pfft*, and her pink bangs fly off her forehead. "I've got to drum up *interest* first."

"You're a force of nature," I tell her. She seriously is. I've never had a friend who has so much in common with a hurricane: loads of wind, utter chaos, and streets lined with debris. On the other hand, Meghan is a lot more fun than a hurricane. So there's that.

"Thank you." She looks at me like I've just crowned her Miss America.

I can't help giving her a little hug. "You're welcome."

The bell rings. "Eek!" Meghan looks at her watch. "Gotta jet. Let me know who else is in!" she calls over her shoulder, as if I've told her that I'm going to help with this project.

Which, of course, I am.

I toss three notebooks into my locker and yank out my history book. I shove what I need for the first two periods into my backpack and slam the locker door shut. Then I dart toward homeroom so quickly that I trip over a pile of books that has just fallen to the floor beside me.

"Watch out!" Artie shouts as I sprawl halfway across the hall, landing on my butt. Eternally sarcastic Ezra bursts into applause, and I give him my best Ms. Lang glare.

"Sorry," Artie mumbles as she begins to gather her books.

I pick up the two spiral notebooks that are closest and hold them out, but Artie has just dropped the other half of her books and a sheaf of homework paper flies into the air like ticker-tape confetti. She has to begin gathering everything all over again. I haul myself off my rear and help.

"Sorry!" Artie says as people push their way past. An eighth grader steps on Artie's notebook, leaving a sneaker mark, and Artie winces.

I pick up the notebook and dust it off while Artie chases down the loose papers. Eventually, we get everything picked up. Artie shoves all of it into her backpack without sorting it, then rubs her temples. "Well, *that* was fun," she snaps.

"You're welcome," I say.

Artie rolls her eyes and starts to walk away.

"What's stressing you?" I ask.

"What?" Artie turns back to face me. "What makes you think I'm stressed?"

"You always get the drops when you're freaking out about something. So what is it?"

The bell for homeroom rings.

"We're late," Artie says.

I shrug. "Anderson gives us two days a semester to be late. I've got two left. How many have you got?"

"Two."

"So now we each have one. What's bugging you?"

Artie sighs and glances down the empty hallway. It's amazing how quickly it clears out. Like, it's complete crowded mayhem for three minutes, then — *bam* — Sahara Desert. "It's just — Improv Group auditions are at lunch today."

"You're trying out?"

"Is that dumb?" Artie bites her lip.

"No, it's fantastic! You'll be terrific. Is that what you're worried about?"

"Well . . . it's just . . . Ms. Lang decides who gets in."

"You'll be great," I tell her. "You're really funny when you want to be." And then, I don't know what makes me do this, but I reach out and touch Artie's hand. She looks surprised, but she squeezes my fingers three times. That was what we always used to do when we were feeling nervous, or whatever. Our secret signal.

Artie closes her eyes, and her chest rises as she takes a deep breath. When she opens her eyes again, they look clearer. Less freaked out. "Thanks, Hayley."

We stand there for a minute, and then I guess we realize that we don't really have anything else to say. So I turn toward homeroom, and Artie follows. I hold the door for her, and we walk in together.

Just like we used to. Back when we were friends.

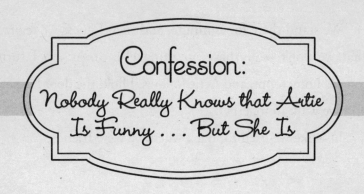

Confession: Nobody Really Knows that Artie Is Funny . . . But She Is

*L*ast year, Artie and I went to see a community theater production of *Annie*. It was, like, the worst show I've ever seen. The lead was pitchy. Daddy Warbucks couldn't dance and looked like he was about twelve. And I couldn't understand a word out of Rooster's mouth.

Artie and I were pretty disappointed, because *Annie* had been our absolute favorite thing in the whole world when we were in second grade. I still love the music. So it was a bummer to see these people butcher it.

Anyway, we went back to my house afterward because Artie was going to spend the night. We headed into the kitchen, and I got out some milk to make cocoa. But the milk slipped out of my hand and spilled all over the floor, and at that moment, Artie busted into "It's a Hard Knock Life," complete with dance routine.

That made me laugh, so she started acting out the whole show. She did all the characters: Annie, Daddy Warbucks, Miss Hannigan, Rooster's girlfriend. Sometime around the song "Maybe," I completely lost it — I was laughing so hard that my sides hurt. I was in pain.

But I still couldn't stop giggling.

I took a sip of water to calm down, and that was when Artie let loose with a spunky rendition of "You're Never Fully Dressed Without a Smile."

Artie tap-danced around the kitchen and got so carried away that she slipped in the spilled milk and landed with a *splat*. Then I snorted my entire drink out of my nose, which made Artie laugh harder. She hauled herself up and tried to collapse on the stool next to me, but she knocked it over instead, and then we both cracked up some more.

We laughed as we cleaned up the kitchen. We laughed as we painted each other's toenails. Then, even after we settled down, one of us would think about it again and start to giggle, then the other one would, too, and soon we were off again.

The laughter even trickled into the next morning, while my dad was making pancakes. Even now, I can't hear a song from *Annie* without cracking up.

I swear to you: That really happened.

It seems like a dream now.

Orange-Creamsicle Cupcakes
(makes approximately 12 cupcakes)

Sometimes, in the middle of winter, I'll just all of a sudden start thinking about summer. Like today, I was looking out at the gray clouds and the snow on the ground, and I started remembering blue skies and walking around without my coat. I thought about the ice cream truck that sometimes comes to our school. And then I wanted a Creamsicle. But it's too cold for a Creamsicle. So — cupcakes!

INGREDIENTS FOR CUPCAKES:
  3/4 cup milk
  1/2 cup orange juice
  1/3 cup canola oil
  3/4 cup granulated sugar
  1 tablespoon orange zest
  1 teaspoon vanilla extract
  1-1/3 cups all-purpose flour
  1 teaspoon baking powder

1/2 teaspoon baking soda

1/4 teaspoon salt

INGREDIENTS FOR ORANGE DRIZZLE (OPTIONAL):

1 cup confectioners' sugar

3/4 teaspoon orange zest

2–4 teaspoons orange juice

INSTRUCTIONS:

1. Preheat the oven to 350°F. Line a muffin pan with cupcake liners.

2. In a large bowl, whisk together the milk, orange juice, oil, sugar, orange zest, and vanilla extract, and set aside.

3. In a separate bowl, sift together the flour, baking powder, baking soda, and salt.

4. Slowly add the dry ingredients to the wet ones a little bit at a time, and combine using a whisk or handheld mixer, until no lumps remain.

5. Fill cupcake liners two-thirds of the way and bake for 20–22 minutes. Transfer to a cooling rack, and let cool completely before frosting.

6. With your (clean!) thumb, poke large holes into the center of each cupcake. Alternately, take a small knife and carve out a cone from the center of each cupcake to create a well. (You can discard the cones, or eat them.)

7. Fill a pastry bag with the vanilla frosting. (You can also make your own pastry bag by cutting off a corner from a plastic Ziploc bag.) Insert the tip of the pastry bag into each cupcake, and squeeze it to fill the cavity you created. Then swirl the frosting on top of the cupcake to cover the opening.

8. OPTIONAL: Prepare the orange drizzle by using a whisk to mix together the confectioners' sugar, orange zest, and orange juice until smooth. Add a little more orange juice if needed to ensure that the mixture has a runny consistency. Drizzle the mixture on top of the vanilla frosting.

Vanilla Frosting

INGREDIENTS:

- 1 cup margarine or butter
- 3-1/2 cups confectioners' sugar
- 1-1/2 tablespoons milk
- 1-1/2 teaspoons vanilla extract

INSTRUCTIONS:

1. In a large bowl, with an electric mixer, cream the margarine or butter until it's a lighter color, about 2–3 minutes.

2. Slowly beat in the confectioners' sugar in 1/2-cup batches, adding a little bit of milk whenever the frosting becomes too thick. Add the vanilla extract and continue mixing on high speed for about 3–7 minutes, until the frosting is light and fluffy.

Wintry Mix

I'm sitting in the window seat, my knees pressed to my chin. I'm trying to read *To Kill a Mockingbird* for English, but it's not working out too well. I really like the book, but I'm having trouble concentrating. Too many thoughts about Chloe and Rupert are floating around in my mind. They're downstairs together now. Rupert is probably playing the piano. Maybe Chloe is reading; maybe she's dancing. Maybe she's just listening, her eyes half-closed.

Outside, the weather is what the forecasters call "a wintry mix," and what I call "disgusting." Rain falls and freezes, making the sidewalks into Slip 'N Slides. The days end early, so it's already almost dark, and the streets are practically deserted. But then I notice a figure almost directly below, taking photographs of the tree outside. The freezing rain has coated the tree with ice, and silver icicles sparkle in the fading light.

The figure is wearing a heavy coat with a hood hiding his face, but I can tell just by the way he's standing there that it's Marco.

That's *so* Marco. To come out in the hideous weather just to photograph a tree. I wonder if he plans to come into the café for a scone or something before he takes the bus back home. I decide to offer him one.

I hop off the window seat and pad out into the hallway in my stockinged feet. My boots are downstairs, beside the door, along with my coat. As I head for the back stairs, I catch Mom's voice on the phone in the kitchen.

"Oh, it's fine," Mom is saying. "I don't know, Denise. It's a bit overwhelming, to tell you the truth."

Denise — that's my aunt. For a moment, I consider asking Mom for the phone. I haven't spoken with my aunt for a few weeks, and she's one of my favorite people in the whole world.

But then Mom says, "There's the girls. It looks like Chloe's best friend is moving away. And the café is picking up, but it's a lot to manage. And now I might have a wedding to plan —"

It's hard to describe what happens to me then. It's like that freezing rain has trickled over my entire body, turning *me* to ice. Wedding?

My feet carry me forward, away from the kitchen, and into the stairwell.

Wedding?wedding?wedding?wedding?wedding? wedding?

I push the word away, sweep it into a corner of my mind. Is Mom planning to marry Ramon? I don't even want to think about it! A few days ago, I was worrying that my dad would get married to Annie. But this would be way weirder. Way.

I step into my boots and pull on my heavy coat, which is still damp from earlier. I grab a red umbrella. I can dimly hear notes from the piano through the mudroom wall. The music fades as I step into the cold. The freezing rain taps like gentle fingertips on my umbrella.

"Hey," I say.

Marco looks over. "Hey," he says. "Everything okay?"

I shrug. "Life is weird," I say.

"Tell me about it," Marco agrees. He looks thoughtful, then snaps a photo of me.

"Oh, jeez, Marco, I must look horrible right now."

"You always look pretty," Marco says.

I feel myself blushing. I'm embarrassed, but Marco clearly isn't. He just looks at me, as if it's perfectly normal to tell someone that they're pretty in the middle of the freezing rain.

Marco kissed me once last year. The moment comes back to me in a rush: my heartbeat as he leaned toward me, the softness of his lips. I'm afraid I might start to cry again, like I did then. Marco gives me another piercing look, and I wonder if he can read my mind. I hope not.

Marco looks away, and says, "Well, I should be getting home."

"Okay," I say. I don't tell him to come inside for a scone.

He tucks the camera into his large pocket and heads off down the street, toward the bus stop.

I think about how Marco snapped that picture of me. I wonder what he saw at that moment. I wonder what that photo will look like, but more than that, I wonder what I look like to him.

*　　*　　*

Chloe hits the MUTE button on the remote control. She always does that during commercials, which drives me a little crazy, to be honest. Chloe complains that commercials are annoying. But when she shuts off the sound, we just sit there watching silent commercials, which is even more annoying.

"I think Jen's going to win," Chloe says, curling her legs beneath her. "Pepe is so full of himself."

"Lots of singers who are full of themselves win this show," I point out.

Chloe sighs. "I know. But I never want them to."

We're on day two of a three-day *American Vocals* finale. Honestly, I don't really know why we bother watching the first two days of this, but we always watch all three. It's Chloe's favorite show.

A detergent commercial flashes up on the screen.

"Mom invited Ramon to dinner this weekend," I say ever-so-casually.

"That's cool."

I'm wondering how to bring up the idea that Mom might be getting married again. "He's pretty nice."

Chloe stares at the silent screen. "Yeah."

I try to imagine watching quiet commercials with Mom on the couch and Ramon in the corner. What kind of stepfather would he be? Strict? Funny? Kind? Boring? What would it be like to have him around all the time?

I just can't picture it.

"Can you imagine Ramon as our stepfather?" I blurt suddenly.

Chloe looks at me with an *Are you on drugs?* look. "Not really," she says. Then she turns the TV's sound back on. "Oh! Pepe's going to sing another one. I hope he messes up. Is that mean?"

"I don't think he can hear you," I tell her.

Chloe giggles and turns to look into my eyes. "Don't worry, Hayley," she says. Then she leans her head on my shoulder.

Guilt pools in my stomach. *I should tell her what I heard,* I think. But it doesn't feel right. Mom should tell us in some kind of official way.

It's funny that just a few nights ago, I thought that Chloe

was freaking out because she thought our father might marry Annie. But she wasn't. And now I really *am* freaking out because our mother might marry Ramon, and Chloe is trying to comfort me.

It's a mixed-up world.

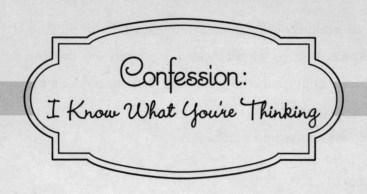

Confession:
I Know What You're Thinking

You're thinking I should've said something.

But maybe I didn't even hear Mom right. Maybe she said, "I have a sledding to plan." As in, a sledding party.

I mean, people say that.

Right?

So why freak Chloe out?

She has enough to deal with.

Artie hums as she sews a button back onto a shirtsleeve. We're back for our fourth afternoon of detention, repairing props and mending costumes. But you wouldn't know it. Both Artie and Meghan are bubbling with enthusiasm.

"Audition went well?" I ask when Artie takes a breath between hums.

She smiles at me. "I think so," she whispers. "Ms. Lang seemed happy with it. I did a lot of scenes with Jamil, who was awesome. Even Chang told me she was really impressed. Joe Jesslyn, too."

Joe Jesslyn is an eighth grader. He's generally known as the funniest guy in the whole school, and he's the only person who ever got into the improv group in the sixth grade. He's head of it now and helps Ms. Lang decide who gets in.

"Well, great," I say, trying to sound enthusiastic. I know that if Artie gets into the improv group, she'll be back in with Chang and her dramarama crew. Well — that's what she wants, I guess. "Have a cupcake." I open the plastic container I have stashed in my bag. "Just don't let Ms. Lang see."

"Thanks!"

"So!" Meghan says brightly as she dumps a stack of shirts onto the table. "I found a whole bunch of shirts that are missing buttons."

"There's a box of spares here," I say, pulling it out. "Let's see what we can match."

"Remember that these costumes just have to look decent on stage," Artie reminds us. "They don't have to match perfectly — people won't see them close up."

"Got it." Meghan sorts through buttons. "Wow, some of these are really pretty. We can use this one for that blouse," she says, selecting a teal blue.

"Have a cupcake," I say. "They're gluten free." Meghan has celiac disease, which means she can't digest gluten. That's a protein in wheat, barley, and some other grains. It's sort of a pain for her, so I try to make stuff she can eat if we're hanging out.

"These are gluten free?" Artie eyes her cupcake suspiciously. "Wow — how did you make them taste so good?"

"It's not that hard," I tell her.

"Hayley's an angel of mercy," Meghan says, taking a bite of the cupcake. "Mmmm!"

"Careful not to get frosting on the costumes," Artie says.

Meghan gives me this heavy-lidded, raised eyebrow look, like, *Who does she think she is?* "I'll be careful," Meghan says, digging her fingers into the buttons again. "Oh, Hayley, I forgot to tell you: Maria's totally in with her juggling act. Kyle is going to play piano. And Chang is going to do a scene with Devon, Trina, and Joe. This talent show is totally coming together!"

Artie looks up from her sewing. Her face has turned a sickly shade of green. Devon was almost her boyfriend for about five minutes . . . until he decided he liked Trina instead. He's a major dramarama, too. All of Artie's so-called friends are doing a scene together . . . and it looks like they forgot to mention it to her.

"Did Ms. Lang say yes to the talent show?" Artie asks.

"Joe says that he thinks he can get her to say yes," Meghan says. She takes another bite of cupcake. "Hey! Hayley, I just got an idea — you should make some cupcakes for the show! Like they do on a cooking show!" She has a bit of icing on the tip of her nose, which makes her look kind of demented. And I'm not even talking about the words coming out of her mouth.

"You can't *bake* at a talent show," Artie snaps. "That's stupid."

"Artie, *you* aren't doing *anything* for the talent show, so you can just shut up," Meghan shoots back.

Artie looks shocked. Then she grabs her leftover cupcake and heaves it at Meghan.

"Whoa!" I shout.

I have to give Meghan credit — the girl can move fast. She ducks, and the cupcake wings right past her ear and splatters on a bust of Socrates behind her.

"Oh, no!" Artie wails, but her remorse costs her — Meghan grabs her own cupcake and tosses it at Artie's face.

Crumbs fly everywhere, and Artie lets out a screech. She reaches for my plastic box of cupcakes, but I yank it away.

Unfortunately, I yank it a little too hard, and cupcakes rain down onto the floor. Frosting first, of course.

For a moment, we all just sit there, staring at the cupcakes. I can hear our breathing, ragged and a little desperate.

"Ms. Lang is coming to check on us any minute," Meghan says.

Artie murmurs, "We are so dead."

I leap off my chair and hurry to the supply closet. I grab an unopened package of paper towels and toss it to Meghan. She yanks off the plastic cover and unrolls a huge wad, which she gives to Artie.

Without a word, Artie wipes off her face while Meghan gets to work on Socrates. I gather the cupcakes from the floor and put them back into the container.

"We can do it!" Meghan says as she races for the broom to tackle the crumbs.

Just then, the door swings open. Ms. Lang stands there for a moment, taking it in — cupcake crumbs everywhere, the chunk of frosting in Artie's hair, the smeary face of Socrates.

"We, um, spilled —" Meghan begins.

"No food in the costume shop!" Ms. Lang barks. She jabs a dagger-like fingernail at a sign near the door. No Food, No Drinks, No Gum in Costume Shop! Ever!

"Sorry," I whisper.

"You three can take an extra day of detention to clean this all up!" Ms. Lang shouts. Then she shoots one last glare at Artie and walks out of the room, slamming the door behind her.

I look over at my Ex-Best. Her face is red, and her eyes brim with tears.

"Artie," I say, "I'm so sorry."

"Please don't talk to me," she whispers. She takes her paper towels and begins to brush the crumbs from the table.

Meghan gets the broom.

For the next thirty-seven minutes, we clean the costume shop in complete silence, until it's time to go home.

The hallway is nearly deserted when I walk out of the costume shop. Meghan is still tidying up, but I have to hurry. I told Gran that I'd help her with some baking at the tea shop when I got home from school.

I hear voices echoing down the hall, and when I round the corner, I see Omar talking to Kyle. Omar has his back to me, but Kyle is wearing his usual beaming smile, patiently explaining his views on the importance of recycling. Behind him, Jamil is doing a weird dance, almost like a chicken, or something. Jamil isn't making any noise, and there isn't any sound, or anything, and it takes me a minute to realize what's going on. Then I notice that Omar is holding up a phone. He's videotaping Kyle's speech — and Jamil's crazy dance behind him.

My blood burns hot, and I feel nauseated and dizzy. I can only imagine what they're doing — making some crazy video of Kyle looking oblivious to a chicken dance. Then they'll put it up on YouTube, and the whole school will get a laugh out of the clueless blind guy.

Want.

To.

Smash!!

Something!!!!!

"What are you doing?" I screech. Omar ducks away, but he's not fast enough. I slap the cell phone out of his hand, and it clatters across the hallway.

"Hey!" Omar shouts. "What's your problem?"

"Hayley?" Kyle asks. He sounds almost afraid, like he thinks maybe I've gone nuts. Which maybe I have.

"If I see that video anywhere, I will beat you with that cell phone," I snarl at Omar, who grimaces in fear.

"We were just kidding around," Jamil says. He, at least, has the decency to look embarrassed. He glances at Kyle, and his dark brown eyes look worried.

"We've been doing this with lots of kids," Omar explains. "Not just Kyle."

"It's different with Kyle, and you know it!" I shout. "And if you don't know it, you should!" I feel like I'm channeling something. I'm not a shouter — I never have been. But this angry thing inside me has taken over. I'm shouting so that I don't start punching.

"Would someone please explain what's going on?" Kyle asks.

"I was just doing a silly dance behind your back," Jamil explains. "Omar was catching the whole thing on video."

Kyle looks baffled. "But what does that have to do with recycling?"

"Nothing," Omar admits. "We just thought it would make a funny video."

Kyle stands there for a moment, almost as if he's taking the words in through his skin. Then he nods, and walks away.

"Kyle!" I call after him.

"I can take care of myself, Hayley," he snaps over his shoulder. The hard stone floors and metal lockers make his voice a tinny echo. And just like that, the angry thing in me whooshes out of my body. It's like I'm a teakettle, and all my hot water has turned to steam, leaving me empty.

Omar walks over to his phone and picks it up. He looks at it thoughtfully for a moment, then looks at me. "It wasn't a big deal, Hayley," he says.

"We didn't mean anything by it," Jamil adds.

"Stop talking," I tell them.

They start down the hall, and someone touches my shoulder gently. It's Meghan. Artie is with her. "We saw that," Meghan says.

"I didn't mean to make Kyle so upset." The hallway blurs and shifts as tears spring to my eyes.

"It's not *your* fault," Artie gripes. "Omar and Jamil are jerks. I'm *glad* you told them off."

"They used to be nice." Meghan shakes her head. "Maybe they just got carried away."

"If I did the right thing, then why do I feel so awful?" I ask.

"What were you supposed to do?" Meghan demands. "Let Omar and Jamil post a video where they make fun of a blind guy? Like, 'Hahaha! He can't see us making fun of him because he's blind — *get it?*' I mean — were you really going to let that happen?"

"Kyle's just embarrassed right now," Artie says gently. "He'll get over it, and he'll realize that you did what friends do."

"What she said," Meghan agrees.

Meghan's eyebrows are knit together beneath her pink bangs. She looks worried. Artie, with her hazel eyes and shiny auburn hair, is wearing the same expression. "Well . . . I guess that if the two of you agree on it, it must be true," I say.

Meghan and Artie exchange a look. Then Meghan cracks up. Artie allows herself this wry little half grin.

"Trust us," Meghan says. "You did the right thing." Then she slings an arm around Artie's shoulder and — for just a minute — I get a flash of how the three of us might be able to get along.

We may never be friends, but it beats tossing cupcakes at one another.

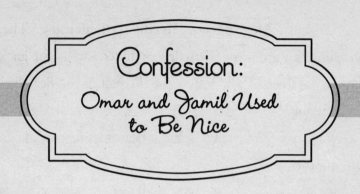

Confession:
Omar and Jamil Used to Be Nice

$\mathcal{I}$ wish someone could stop those guys.

Omar and Jamil have always been funny. They used to sit at the back of the bus, rapping about homework or the food in the cafeteria.

But lately, they've started picking on people to get laughs. The other day, on the bus, they somehow managed to steal Jackson Jackson's T-shirt. They yanked it right over his head and threw it out the window. Everyone on the bus started shouting and the driver stopped the bus, and JJ had to go down the aisle shirtless and into the street to get it. Half the kids were doubled over with laughter. The other half were taking pictures of JJ with their cell phones.

Here's the thing — JJ is scrawny. He's a sixth grader, but he looks more like a fourth grader. Not only is he puny, but he always wears these big, baggy clothes, like he's wearing the size he thinks he ought to have on but can't quite fit into. Or maybe it's just a hip-hop look. Either way, he's usually swimming in his shirts so you can't really tell how small he is.

But that day, with his shirt off, you could see the bones in his chest. When he walked down the aisle, I saw his spine, like a row of buttons down the center of his back. When he got back on the bus, his face was burning red, and he looked like he was about to burst into tears. I don't know if he was humiliated or furious or both.

I would've been both.

JJ sat in the front of the bus and didn't speak to anyone for the rest of the ride. He hasn't been back on the bus for two weeks.

The thing is, I don't actually believe that Omar and Jamil are mean. They just don't know when to stop. They'll do anything for a laugh.

Which, when you really think about it, is kind of terrifying.

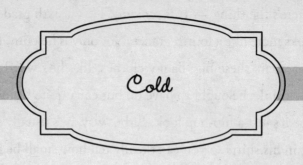

Cold

It's almost five o'clock and nearly pitch-black as I make my way down the hill into town. My brain is still buzzing from the whole Kyle scene. I feel horrible that I've embarrassed him. I didn't mean to. I wonder if I should apologize, and if so, what I should say.

Snow has been piled into the center of the street, creating a wall along the median so that you can hardly see the shops on the other side. Most of the businesses shovel their walks thoroughly, but I am still careful as I pick my way along the concrete. You can go sprawling if you hit a patch of ice.

I look up at the Academy of Music marquee, which screams into the darkness with brilliant red lettering. Tonight!

METROPOLIS — FULLY RESTORED! The poster by the door shows a black-and-white mechanical man surrounded by Saturn-like rings of light. Some silent movie, I guess. I'm surprised by how many people are in line. I mean, if I wanted to hear people not talk, I could go to the library for free.

The crowd is mostly older, but I spot Marco in the middle of the line.

Warmth floods through my cold body. "Marco!" I shout, waving. It strikes me that luck has sent him my way. After all, Marco is Kyle's friend. Maybe he'll have a good idea about what I should say to him.

Marco looks over and waves to me. I hurry to join him. The line is fidgety, but not moving forward; they haven't opened the doors yet.

"Hey!" I say, and I'm aware that I'm beaming wider than usual as Marco grins back.

"Are you here for the movie?" Marco asks.

"No, I — what is it?"

"What is it?" Marco repeats.

The person in front of him turns around. It's Tanisha Osborne, our class Know-It-All. She's wearing a green knit cap with earflaps and an enormous pink flower plastered on it. Long black braids stick out from the sides. The close-fitting cap emphasizes her large brown eyes fringed with black lashes, and, honestly, she looks prettier than I've ever seen her. "It's the Fritz Lang classic," Tanisha says. "One of the most important movies ever made."

"Oh," I say. "Have you seen it?"

"Four times, but never on the big screen." She looks up at the marquee reverently.

"I've only seen it once," Marco says. He pulls a couple of M&M'S out of the bag he's holding and crunches them. "It's amazing. When Tanisha told me it was coming to the Academy of Music, we got tickets right away."

We *got tickets? They're here together?* "Oh," I say again, feeling like an idiot. Would you like to buy a vowel? I seem to have an *O*. "I didn't know you were into silent movies." I'm not even sure who I'm saying this to — Marco or Tanisha. I didn't know *anyone* was into silent movies.

"I love classic cinema," Tanisha says in that way she has that always makes people kind of want to slap her.

"I've gotten really into it ever since I've been using the

video camera," Marco explains. "Some of the techniques in these old movies are really amazing."

"Marco has an incredible eye for capturing images in a frame," Tanisha says.

"She's teaching me," Marco explains, and then I remember that Tanisha is Marco's math tutor. And apparently now she's his video tutor, too.

Marco holds out the bag of M&M'S, and Tanisha yanks off her glove and dips her fingers in. She pulls out a couple of candies and pops them into her mouth. For some reason, this makes me feel a little sick. I can't believe I didn't even realize that Marco and Tanisha were becoming friends. Well, why shouldn't they? "Want some?" Marco asks, offering me the bag.

"No, thanks," I start to say, but my voice gets caught in my throat. I clear it and try again, but at that moment, the line starts to move forward.

Marco moves up beside Tanisha, who pulls a pair of tickets out of her pocket. "Sure you don't want to join?" he asks, looking back at me.

"It's sold-out," Tanisha tells him. Again, I kinda want to smack her.

"That's okay," I call after them. "I've got to get home to help Gran." But they are already swept into the crowd, moving away from me.

In the next moment, Marco is through the doors, already gone.

I never even got to ask him about Kyle.

Confession:
I Don't Want Marco to Have a Girlfriend

The night that Artie told me she had a crush on Marco, I couldn't sleep. This was a year and a half ago, but it's one of those memories that I've played over in my mind so often that it feels shiny and new, like a penny that has been rubbed clean.

We were in my room, back when I had my own room. I was in my bed; Artie was on the trundle, and she asked if I could keep a secret. Then she told me that she liked Marco.

Like liked him.

I felt as if I'd just been hit by lightning, or maybe just whacked in the head with something heavy. I was stunned. And I said something dumb, like, "What if he doesn't like you back? That would be weird."

But it would've been even weirder if he *had* liked her back.

I mean, where would that have left me? If my two best friends became boyfriend and girlfriend, what would I be?

Leftovers.

I remember staring up at my ceiling, which was covered in glow-in-the-dark stars. Marco and Artie had helped me stick them up there. "These are pretty heavy plastic," Marco had said as he stuck a fat one directly over my pillow. "If it falls down while you're asleep, we could be talking major brain damage."

"You're hilarious, Marco," I'd told him.

"The plastic isn't that heavy," Artie had pointed out. "Besides, Hayley has a pretty thick skull."

I wondered what putting up the stars would've been like if Artie and Marco had been sneaking giggles at each other the whole time. Or trying to hold hands. Or out watching a movie together, while I stuck the stars up by myself.

And then, a few weeks later, my parents announced they were getting divorced. I went out in the backyard and told Marco about it. He comforted me. Then he kissed me.

Then I burst into tears.

I didn't know what to do with that kiss. I didn't want to be Marco's girlfriend, either. That would have been just as weird as Artie being his girlfriend — maybe even weirder. It would have messed everything up.

But, as you know, things got messed up, anyway.

Just when things were seeming kind of normal again, Tanisha entered the picture.

It looks like we're never going back to normal.

I guess that isn't a real place, anyway.

Lemon-Ginger Cupcakes

(makes approximately 12 cupcakes)

I read that *basil* means "best wishes," and I like the idea of taking flavors that are sour and strong (lemon and ginger) and making them sweet. These are my Forgiveness cupcakes. I hope they work.

INGREDIENTS:

    1 cup milk

    1 teaspoon apple cider vinegar

    1-1/4 cups all-purpose flour

    1 tablespoon cornstarch

    3/4 teaspoon baking powder

    1/2 teaspoon baking soda

    1/2 teaspoon salt

    1/3 cup canola oil

    3/4 cup granulated sugar

    1 teaspoon vanilla extract

    2-1/2 teaspoons ground ginger

    Zest from 1 large lemon

INSTRUCTIONS:

1. Preheat the oven to 350°F. Line a muffin pan with cupcake liners.

2. In a large bowl, whisk together the milk and vinegar, and set aside for a few minutes to curdle.

3. In a separate bowl, sift together the flour, cornstarch, baking powder, baking soda, and salt.

4. Once the milk has curdled, whisk in the oil, sugar, vanilla extract, ground ginger, and lemon zest. Then slowly add the dry ingredients to the wet ones a little bit at a time, and combine using a whisk or handheld mixer, stopping to scrape the sides of the bowl a few times, until no lumps remain.

5. Fill cupcake liners two-thirds of the way and bake for 18–20 minutes. Transfer to a cooling rack, and let cool completely before frosting.

Basil Cream-Cheese Frosting

INGREDIENTS:

- 1/4 cup margarine or butter
- 1/4 cup cream cheese, softened
- 2 cups confectioners' sugar
- 1 teaspoon vanilla extract
- 1 tablespoon minced fresh basil leaves

INSTRUCTIONS:

1. In a large bowl, with an electric mixer, cream together the margarine or butter and cream cheese until completely combined, about 2–3 minutes.

2. Slowly beat in the confectioners' sugar in 1/2-cup batches, adding the vanilla extract about halfway through. Once all the sugar has been added, mix in the minced basil. Continue mixing the frosting on high speed for about 3–7 minutes, until the frosting is light and fluffy. It's best to make the frosting a day ahead to allow the flavor to really come out.

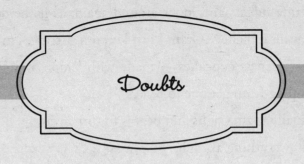

Doubts

The bell over the door jingles and a figure draped in black fabric bustles in. Cold air claws its way into the warm bakery before Uzma has a chance to shut the door.

"Hullo," Gran says, but her blue eyes are wary.

Uzma's dark eyes flash around the café. Mrs. McTibble sits at a corner table, sharing a scone with her "service dog," Gwendolyn. (Gwendolyn wears a jacket that says "service dog" on it, so we have to let her in the café, but she's also a Lhasa Apso, so I have my doubts.) A few students are drinking coffee and studying at the long table, and people on laptops are scattered about. "Have you seen Umer?" Uzma blurts.

"Not since he dropped off the flowers earlier today," Gran admits.

Uzma fidgets and looks around again, as if she doesn't quite want to believe Gran. I just keep on stirring. I'm making Forgiveness cupcakes — made with lemon and ginger. I'm hoping I can get one to Kyle.

Finally, Uzma sighs and begins to turn away.

"Is everything all right?" Gran asks.

Uzma cocks her head, clearly surprised. "Yes, thank you," she says sharply. There's an edge in her voice. It definitely sounds like something is not all right. I look over at Gran, and see her right eyebrow lift slightly.

"Would you like a cupcake?" Gran asks her.

"No, thank you." Uzma's tone is as cold as the frigid February air outside.

"Oh, come now, I insist," Gran says. "Hayley has just made a fresh batch, haven't you, dear? Surely you won't refuse my granddaughter's recipe?" She unties her apron and comes out from behind the counter, smiling her most engaging smile. "Hayley, dear, would you mind bringing us each a cupcake? And perhaps a pot of tea?" Gran takes Uzma by the arm and steers her toward the table by the bay window. "Is Earl Grey all right?"

"That would be lovely," Mr. Malik's sister replies a little uncertainly. I mean, who can say no to Gran when she's being so charming — and forceful.

I get out two plates and set a cupcake on each. Then I pour some hot water into a teapot. I take over the cupcakes and then come back for the tea. When I return, Uzma is telling Gran about her ungrateful nephew, and Gran is nodding sympathetically. I think about what Mr. Malik said — that his sister needs a project — and wonder if Gran might be able to help her out.

Maybe we could teach her to make cupcakes, or something.

When I turn around, there's a customer standing at the counter. "Rupert, how did you sneak in without jingling the bell?" I ask him.

Rupert shrugs. "Is Chloe home?"

What is this? The lost and found? Why is everyone looking for someone today? "Actually, she's out shopping with Mom," I tell him.

"Okay." He looks over the treats in the glass case.

"Rupert, can I ask you something? Chloe tells me that you're moving away. Is that true?"

Rupert tears his eyes away from the profiteroles. "Just across town."

"But you're changing schools?"

He looks away. "Yes."

"But — you know — Northampton has school choice. You can choose where you go."

Rupert sighs. "I know. You can choose your school. But that doesn't mean they'll send a school bus out to get you. If you want to go to a school you're not zoned for, you have to have someone take you. And my dad's job starts early in the morning. He can't drive me."

"Oh." I wonder if Gran or Mom could take Rupert. But no. The café is always super busy in the morning. We open at six A.M. "Are you . . . How do you feel about living with your father?"

"I love my dad," Rupert says, and his voice is so warm that it actually surprises me. Chloe's best friend isn't exactly the most expressive guy.

"Well . . . we'll miss having you so close."

"I know," Rupert says, and his eyes travel to the floor. "I'll miss Chloe. And the Daczewitzes."

"Who are they?"

"My foster family."

"Oh." I flash back to a memory of Rupert at Halloween, with his sisters. I noticed at the time that they were much older, and that they looked completely different from him. *You can never predict a family*, Gran had said then.

"Mr. Daczewitz is my dad's good friend, from when they were in the National Guard together," Rupert explains. "He said he'd take care of me, while my dad went . . . away."

"Where did he go?" The minute I ask, I want to take the words back. *Where the heck do you think he went, Hayley? On a Caribbean vacation?* "You don't have to answer that," I add quickly.

"It's okay. He was in a residential treatment program." Rupert's shoulder rises and dips. "He made some bad friends."

"Got it." Residential treatment. That means drugs or alcohol. A shiver goes through me as I imagine what that must have been like.

"It's not what you're thinking. He was never bad to me. He just messed up his life."

"I wasn't thinking anything." *Sometimes it's okay to tell a bald-faced lie*, I say to myself.

The door blasts open again, and there's Chloe. Her cheeks are pink, her eyes shining. Mom is behind her, carrying a canvas tote bag full of groceries.

"Rupie!" Chloe shouts and races up to join us. "Are you here to work on our book?"

"I was a little early," Rupert admits. "I was just talking to Hayley."

If Chloe catches the strained note in his voice, she doesn't say so. "Let's head up to my room," she says. "I've got a few new ideas. . . ."

Neither one of them looks back at me as they scurry toward the back stairs.

"Hayley, would you put these into the fridge?" Mom asks, pulling out whole milk and cream for the café. "I'm heading upstairs to start dinner."

"Sure," I say, and bend down to tuck everything into the tiny fridge under the counter.

"Well, thank you for a lovely chat," I hear Uzma say.

"It was a pleasure," Gran replies. "Come by anytime."

I straighten up just in time to see the oddest sight ever: Uzma awkwardly embracing Gran, who can't really hug back due to (a) extreme surprise and (b) the fact that she's holding a dirty plate in each hand.

Uzma finally releases her and blasts out the doorway in her graceless way.

"Well," Gran says as she places the dishes into the tub we use to bus the tables. "That was interesting. And how was your chat with Rupert?"

"I'm not sure." I explain a little bit about his situation. "I think I shouldn't have asked so many questions. I might have hurt his feelings."

"Mmm. Perhaps," Gran says as she pulls out a jar of colorful candy-covered sesame seeds. She places a few on the top of my cupcake, so that it looks like a flower. Sometimes, I forget that my grandmother is a genius when it comes to baked treats. "But maybe Rupert wanted to tell someone what's going on in his life." She glances out the window, and I wonder if it's Rupert she's thinking of, or Uzma. "Sometimes the people who most want to share are the ones who aren't very good at it. Well . . . until they get going."

"Rupert's interesting to talk to," I say.

Gran smiles at me. "Yes, that's what Chloe tells me."

I laugh. I know what Gran is really saying — I used to be worried that Rupert was strange, and I wanted Chloe to make a "normal" friend. But now I know that Rupert and Chloe are perfect for each other. They're just shy. And smart. And sweet.

I really wish he wasn't moving away.

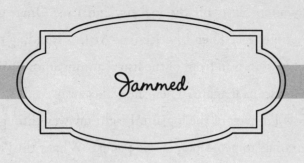

Jammed

There is some sort of major logjam in the hallway that's slowing everyone down. I look at my watch. If people don't pick up the pace, I'll be late to math. Great. Mr. Carter loves any excuse to give people detention.

As I near the drama room, I see the problem: There's a crowd gathered around a piece of paper posted by the door. The dramaramas are blocking the traffic. I spot my old crush, Devon, peering at the list, but I don't say hello or try to catch his eye. It actually makes me a little sick to look at him now. How could I ever have thought he was cute? Sure, he looks like a lip-balm model — but he's kind of a jerk. Besides, his left ear is bigger than his right.

A whoop blasts off the lockers, and I see Omar giving Jamil a high five. Then I notice that Artie is standing beside them. She stands in front of the list, scanning it for a minute. Then she scans it again. Then she walks away.

Now I'm part of the logjam. I fight my way through the dramaramas to get a look at the paper. "What's this?" I ask Jamil, who's still hanging around, grinning.

"Improv callbacks," he says.

I feel like he has just reached into my chest and squeezed my heart. I scan the list. Trina Bachman's name is there. Omar. Jamil. Devon.

Artie's name isn't there.

I look down the hall. I can still see her flowered back-pack. "Excuse me," I say as I push through the crowd. "Artie!" I call. "Artemis!"

I know she can hear me, but she doesn't turn back. But the crowd is thinning out, so I break into a jog. "Artie," I say, and I touch her shoulder.

She freezes, and I get in front of her to block her way. Artie's face is red, and a thin blue vein in her forehead is standing out. Her eyes are red, too, and I know she's focusing all of her will on not crying.

"I'm sorry," I tell her.

Artie sucks in some air. "No big deal," she says brightly. "Lots of people didn't make it." She even manages to smile, but she's looking over my shoulder.

She really is a good actress, I realize. "It *is* a big deal," I say.

Artie's hazel eyes meet mine. "You don't have to pretend to care," she says. Then she steps around me, like I'm something in the way. A stone, maybe.

And I can't really tell if I do care or not.

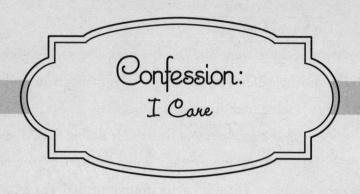

Confession:
I Care

I used to have a hamster named Fabio. He had long, golden fur and a twitchy little nose. He loved cantaloupe and going outside in the backyard. I loved the feel of his scratchy little feet as he tried to run up and down my arm.

Anyway, I had Fabio for three and a half years, and then, two weeks after Christmas, he died. I don't know why. I didn't feed him anything weird, or forget about him. He just died, I guess. I still feel sad when I think about it.

I cried for a long time after Dad buried Fabio in the backyard. Mom and Dad tried to cheer me up, but I could tell that they didn't really think I should be so upset over a hamster.

I told Marco about Fabio, and he said, "That's sad. Hamsters don't live very long." He was nice, but I could tell he didn't really want to talk about Fabio.

When I told my friends Lily and Jane at school, Jane just shrugged and started talking about her fish. Lily said her parents wouldn't let her have any pets, and that was the end of the conversation.

Chloe was the only person who seemed to feel the way I did. She bawled her head off. But that didn't really make me feel better.

And then there was Artie. When I told her about Fabio, she looked . . . I don't know . . . stricken. I think that's the word. Like someone had just slapped her. She grabbed my hand and said, "Oh!" and then she have me a big hug. "Are you okay?" she asked.

"I'm sad," I said.

"Of course you are," Artie told me, like it was the most obvious thing in the world. Like it was normal to be sad over a hamster.

"I'm *really* sad," I confessed. My voice was almost a whisper. It was hard to get the words out.

"Fabio lived with you in your room for three years!" Artie cried. "He was there every day! You played with him, you fed him, you petted him. You spent more time with Fabio than with anyone else!"

And then I really did start to cry, and Artie hugged me. I cried really hard until I started to hiccup, and Artie rubbed my back until I calmed down.

I guess big deals are relative. What may be a big deal to one person isn't a big deal to another. Or maybe some people are good at handling one kind of big deal, and bad at handling others. When my parents announced that they were splitting up, Artie didn't want to talk about it. She wasn't a very good friend then.

But when Fabio died, she hugged me while I cried. Then we went outside together, into the snowy yard. I showed Artie the place where we had buried him, and she sang "Amazing Grace," and we talked about the time Fabio got lost in the hosta plants and Marco wanted to call 911 for help. (We wouldn't let him, and we found Fabio about three minutes later.) I remembered the funny little squeaks he would make when he was happy, and Artie remembered the time that he was crawling on my shoulder and dug his way into my shirt.

We talked and laughed for a long time, and by the time Artie went home, I felt like the pieces of my heart had knit back together a little bit.

Artie was the only person who knew it was a really big deal when my hamster died.

And I know it's a really big deal that she didn't make the callback list for the improv group.

Here is a secret: Sometimes you don't stop caring about someone just because they aren't nice to you.

It would be easier if you could.

Come Together

"I just can't figure out if we should open with juggling, or with David Lesser and his Corgi," Meghan says as she stirs her yogurt.

"What does David's Corgi do?" I ask. I've met Priscilla — she's a great dog, but her legs are so short and stubby that I can't imagine her jumping through a hoop, or anything.

"She does ballet, apparently," Meghan says.

"Are you joking right now?"

"No."

"No, really. Tell the truth."

"I am."

"Quit lying."

"Swear," Meghan says, holding up three fingers, scouts-honor style. "David says she dances on her hind legs."

"Open with that," I say, and nibble a plantain chip. I seriously love them. The salty kind, not the sweet ones.

Meghan nods, makes a note, then takes a bite of her yogurt. "This talent show is really coming together."

"Have you asked Ms. Lang's permission yet?"

"Not exactly." Meghan blows her pink bangs out of her eyes.

I sigh. I should have known.

"If everything's all set, it'll be harder for her to say no," Meghan reasons.

"If everything's all set, it'll be easier for her to go ballistic," I shoot back.

Meghan chews on her pen cap. "Do you think it's possible to do it without her finding out?"

"No. And if you try, Meghan Markerson, I swear, you can forget about my help."

"Okay, okay." She rolls her eyes and makes another note. "Too bad Artie won't help us. She could probably convince Ms. Lang to go for it."

It's as if the mention of Artie's name causes her to appear. I see her cross the cafeteria and approach the dramarama table holding her tray. She hovers at the end for a moment, and I think that she and I realize at the same moment that there isn't an open seat for her. Artie glances over at the other nearby chairs, as if she might drag one over, but nobody at the table even looks at her. I see her mouth move, forming, "Hey."

Still nobody glances her way.

"Okay, I'm thinking that Adelaide Green's jazz trio can open the second half," Meghan is saying, but I'm barely listening. I can't tear my eyes away from the train wreck happening at the dramarama table. Artie hesitates a moment, uncertain. Chang finally looks over at her. But that's all she does. She eyeballs Artie from head to foot, then turns back to Trina Bachman. Sharp little needles stick into my heart as Artie turns and walks toward the double doors.

"Where are you going?" Meghan calls, and that's when I realize that I'm chasing Artie. I don't even remember deciding to go after her. I'm just doing it.

"Artie?" I ask softly once I'm two steps behind her.

She wheels, her eyes flashing. "How many times do I have to ask you to call me Artemis?" she snaps.

"Um — one more?"

She huffs out a sigh, and her nostrils flare. "What do you want, Hayley?" she asks. She sounds tired.

"I just wondered if you wanted to eat lunch with me and Meghan," I say.

Artie blushes, and I wonder if maybe I shouldn't have let her know that I saw her get dissed by the dramaramas. "Sit with the two of you?" she hisses. Her eyes fill, and a tear catches on her long eyelashes. "Are you serious? This whole thing is your fault!"

I almost walk away. Almost. But, for some reason, my feet stay bolted to the floor. The usual noise of the cafeteria surrounds us — the clank and chatter of lunch. It reminds me of the café, and I find myself thinking of Gran and Uzma.

Sometimes the people who most want to share are the ones who aren't very good at it, Gran had said.

"Yeah, I get that," I say to Artie. "But — maybe you want to sit with us, anyway."

Artie stares at me for a moment. She sneaks a sideways glance toward the drama table and presses her lips together, so that they form a slim seam. She doesn't need to speak.

I turn and walk back to my table. Artie is right behind me.

"Oh." Meghan's eyebrows are raised in surprise as Artie places her tray on our table. "Hi."

Artie doesn't reply. She looks down at her food. Her face is hidden by a curtain of auburn hair, but I see a teardrop spill into her salad.

Meghan pulls a crumpled tissue out of her bag.

Artie looks at it, then takes it. "Thank you," she whispers.

I pick up the cupcake from my tray and place it on Artie's.

My Ex-Best blows her nose and then takes a bite of the cupcake. "This is really good," she says after a moment. Her voice is quiet and she doesn't look up when she says it. That's okay.

She doesn't have to say anything else.

I know she means more than the cupcake.

The final bell rang ten minutes ago, and I'm walking down the hall toward the costume shop when I hear piano notes floating from one of the practice rooms. They're so beautiful, I feel like I can catch them in midair, like butterflies.

I'm pretty sure I know who's playing, but I peek as I walk by, anyway. I pause in the doorway.

It's Kyle.

His fingers are long and slim, and almost as pale as the ivory keys they dance across. I tuck my hair behind my ear and hitch my book bag higher onto my shoulder, wishing I knew what to say to him. I want to apologize. I also want him to understand that he shouldn't be embarrassed — it's not his fault that Jamil and Omar are jerks.

But I also kind of want to just walk away.

"I hope you're enjoying this, whoever you are," Kyle announces. He doesn't turn his head toward the door frame, and I wonder how he knows I'm here. Maybe I'm blocking some of the light.

This is my last chance to escape unnoticed. I don't take it.

"It's Hayley," I tell him.

His fingers pause for just a moment, then he plays on. "Hi," he says. The keys at the top of the keyboard tinkle.

"What are you playing?" I ask, mostly because I can't think of anything else to say.

Kyle shrugs. "Just something I made up. Well, I'm still working on it." He plays a few more notes, then pushes himself away from the keys.

"You're making it up?"

"I was thinking of playing it at the talent show."

"You know that might not be a real thing, right? I mean, Meghan hasn't told anyone in the administration that it's happening. She hasn't even reserved the auditorium."

Kyle's smile is lopsided. "She'll work it out."

"You're probably right."

"She has freaky powers," Kyle says. "People do what she asks."

I laugh a little, but it comes out like a snort. "Tell me about it."

Kyle scoots over on the piano bench, and I come and sit down beside him. His fingers stray over the keys a little as he plays a simple melody from the song he was creating a moment before.

"That's really beautiful," I tell him.

"Thanks," Kyle says. His fingers drop from the keys.

Neither one of us speaks.

His arm shifts, and it presses against mine for a moment. I don't move mine away, and he doesn't move his, either.

My whole head starts to tingle. I can hear myself breathe.

Kyle turns toward me. "I'm sorry," he says.

"Why?" The word is a whisper. I don't mean it to be, but I can't quite catch my breath.

"I didn't mean to be so — I don't know. That whole Jamil and Omar thing . . . That wasn't your fault. I didn't mean to get mad at you."

"I know," I say, even though I didn't know, not until he said so.

"Those guys aren't so bad. . . ."

"They've just gone crazy lately," I agree.

"Yeah." Kyle sighs, and I feel his breath against my arm. His eyes are the gray of a deep ocean beneath a stormy sky. "I wish —" he says, then breaks off.

"What?"

He smiles, but it's a sad smile. "I just wish I could see your face right now, Hayley," Kyle says.

His arm is still warm against mine. I forget to breathe.

"Hayley Hicks, what are you doing in here?" Ms. Lang screeches from the doorway.

I jump from the bench, like electricity has just shot through me. "Oh!"

"You're supposed to be in detention! You're late! You'll stay an extra twenty minutes!" She's like a car alarm.

"Okay, okay," I tell her. "Fine." And just like that, I scramble out of the practice room. Ms. Lang is right on my heels.

I don't say good-bye to Kyle. I don't even look back.

I feel as if my hair was on fire and Ms. Lang just doused me with a bucket of water.

But I'm not sure that I'm grateful.

Confession:
What Just Happened?

What did that mean? Why did he want to see my face? Why do I feel so dizzy?

Do I have a crush on Kyle? I don't know.

When I used to see Devon, I'd feel tongue-tied and shy. I'd get clumsy and say stupid stuff.

I'm not like that with Kyle. When I'm with him, I just feel kind of . . . happy. The way you do around a friend.

Except I don't feel that way around my other friends.

Just Kyle.

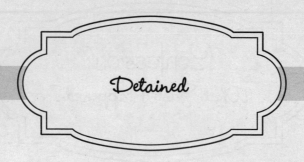

Detained

Today's assignment: script highlighting.

Yes. That's right. My detention "job" is to take a highlighter and mark everything that the character Mr. Wallings says in the script for a play called *Laugh Tracks*. When that's finished, I get to take the next script and highlight everything Mrs. Wallings says. Then I get to highlight a script for Pesky Stahl.

It's a thrill.

"This play is *so* bad," Meghan says as she flips through a script. "Seriously, my cat could write a better play."

"I think it's funny," Artie says.

Meghan rolls her eyes. "'Something's fishy,'" she reads

from the script. " 'Oh, darling, that's just the salmon I cooked for dinner.' " She purses her lips in Artie's direction.

"Maybe it's all in the delivery," I say.

Artie doesn't say anything. She just marks up her page and flips it over.

"All I know is that the dramaramas are going to perform an original improv at the talent show, and I'll bet it will be fifty times funnier than this play," Meghan says.

Artie scowls and flips another page. It's an angry page-flip, if you know what I mean. Crinkly.

Meghan is completely oblivious to Artie's furious highlighting. "So, listen, I think I'm going to talk to Ms. Lang today."

"Finally," I say.

"Don't do it," Artie puts in.

"Why not?"

Artie snaps the cap back onto her highlighter and looks at Meghan evenly. "Because it's going to be a huge disaster."

"What's going to be a huge disaster?" Ms. Lang asks as she walks into the costume shop. She narrows her eyes at me, and I look down at my script and highlight the first thing I see. Shoot. Wrong line.

"Ms. Lang, I've been learning a lot by spending time in the drama department," Meghan says in her Teacher Hypnotist voice. I've heard her use this tone before — teachers and administrators seem to find it soothing. They usually agree to whatever she suggests.

Ms. Lang doesn't seem hypnotized, though. She folds her arms across her chest. "Really," she says.

"Yes! And I've been thinking — there's so much talent here at Adams Middle School. Wouldn't it be great if we could do a talent show?" Meghan's eyes are shining, and I feel my heart pulsing against my chest.

Ms. Lang shakes her head. "I've got enough to do," she says.

"Oh, but a talent show doesn't take much prep or rehearsal, because everyone just brings the talent they've already got," Meghan explains. "The kids who've signed up are —"

"Signed up?" Ms. Lang snaps.

"Well, uh — I haven't really signed them up exactly . . ." Meghan looks over at me for help, but all I can do is wince.

"You do realize that you need permission from this department to use the stage, don't you?" Ms. Lang glares at Meghan.

"Yes, of course — I just thought —"

"You thought that I'd love your brilliant idea as much as you do?" The drama teacher's voice is scornful. "Yes, who wouldn't, Meghan?" she demands sarcastically. "What teacher wouldn't be thrilled to take on more work in order to humor you?"

Meghan's cheeks are flushed. She opens her mouth to speak but doesn't make a sound. I've never seen her speechless before — it's a little unnerving. She looks at me again. I don't know what to say.

"Well, Meghan was just so excited because she thought it would be a good fund-raiser for the Appletree Foundation," Artie says suddenly.

For a moment, Ms. Lang doesn't tear her eyes away from Meghan. It's like it takes a while for Artie's words to settle over her. Finally, she cocks her head and looks over at Artie. "Fund-raiser?" she repeats.

"Right," Artie chirps. "Since you're on the board of directors for Appletree, we thought you might be interested."

We? I look at Artie in surprise.

Artie doesn't glance at me, though. She's looking at Meghan.

"Oh, right!" Meghan says. "You know, art for a good cause," she says brightly.

"Hmm." Ms. Lang runs her index finger over her right eyebrow. "Well, that's a bit different, isn't it? Actually, that's a good idea. Yes."

"The three of us have already done a lot of the legwork," Artie says. "You know, just in case you said yes. But lots of the kids are really excited about it. Especially David Lesser."

"David Lesser?" Ms. Lang repeats.

"His dog does ballet," Meghan puts in.

Oh, Artie, you evil genius. Everyone knows that the Lessers are loaded. Ms. Lang's eyes go wide, and I can almost see the dollar signs in them. Appletree is a nonprofit that brings arts classes to homeless teens. I've heard that Ms. Lang is really passionate about it, but it doesn't have a big budget.

"Well, girls, I think this is a good idea. An excellent idea. Once you finish up the scripts, you can work on putting the talent show together. When were you thinking of holding it, Meghan?"

"Friday after next," Meghan says.

"Ambitious." Ms. Lang frowns.

"Like I said, no rehearsal, no problem." Meghan smiles her charming smile.

"Well, you have my permission to move forward," Ms. Lang says. Then she strides out of the costume shop.

Meghan gives Artie a hilarious fish-lipped, lifted-eyebrow look. "Well, that was amazing," she says.

"I couldn't just sit here watching you two squirm," Artie shoots back. She looks at me and shakes her head.

"Besides, you know this is going to be super fun!" I tell her.

Artie looks at me. Then she laughs a little. "Yeah, Hayley," she says. "It's going to be fun."

I can't help smiling. I actually really think it will be.

Fun, I mean.

Talent

"What do you think?" Artie asks Monday morning in homeroom. She holds up a glittery poster that reads, ADAMS SCHOOL TALENT SHOW. IF YOU'VE GOT IT, WE WANT TO SEE IT, in glittery letters. There's a sign-up sheet at the bottom.

"Perfect!" Meghan gushes.

"I submitted the info for the morning announcements," I say just as the PA system starts to crackle.

"Sit down, everyone," Ms. Anderson says in a bored voice. "Take a seat. Listen up."

"I'll put this up in the drama wing," Artie says as she rolls up the poster.

"Front hall is better," Meghan tells her. "More people will see it."

Artie just cocks an eyebrow, and I know that the poster is going up in the drama wing.

"Good morning, fellow students," blares from the PA. It's the president of the eighth-grade class council, Gia Andres. "It's Monday, February 27. All students who wish to participate in this spring's election should attend an orientation . . ."

Meghan passes me a note. Have a few ideas for talent show. Talk at lunch?

I fold it over and write back. Let's talk at detention so Artie can join.

Okay. Last day — yay!

I look over and grin. I've been waiting to get that extra hour back in the afternoon. Which I'll now be spending planning the talent show, of course.

The PA drones on. ". . . and finally, anyone interested in signing up for the talent show —"

Meghan puts out a thumbs-up.

"— should sign up — Hey! What are you —"

Oh, no. A familiar voice — make that two familiar voices — plow over the sound system.

"This is Jamil —"

"And Omar!"

"And we're here to rhyme!"

"So pardon us for busting up announcement time!"

Meghan looks over at me. Her eyes are dangerous slits. "I'm going to throttle them," she murmurs.

I catch Artie's eye from across the room. She's shaking her head.

I roll my eyes. Great. My announcement got rap-bombed. I'd spent a lot of time writing it, too.

If Meghan wants to throttle those guys, I think, *she's going to have to get in line.*

A Fine Mess

"We're getting too many sign-ups," Artie says as she brushes a green wig. The costume shop is really looking good. It's our last day of detention, and at least it's served some purpose. The racks are hung with clothes that are clean and repaired, everything organized by size and color. The tables are stacked with props, the hats are in boxes or displayed on shelves. "We should weed a few people out."

"Weed a few people out?" Meghan looks aghast, which is kind of hilarious, given that she's wearing a black pillbox hat with cherries on it. "Why should we weed people out?"

Artie lifts an eyebrow. "Um, because some of these acts sound horrible?" She puts down her wig and scans the list. "What's an 'Umbrella Dance'?"

"But isn't the fun of a talent show the fact that some of the acts are bad?" I ask as I put another stitch into the cape I'm working on. It's purple velvet, and I'm repairing some gold trim at the edges. I can't decide if it's gorgeous or hideous. Both, kind of.

Artie looks ready to strangle me with the green wig. "If we let everyone in, the show will be three hours long!"

"Not if we only give everyone three minutes to perform," I say. "That's what we were counting on, right?"

"I told Seth that he could have five," Meghan puts in. "And your act might take a little longer."

"My *act*?" I repeat.

"You're going to make cupcakes, right?" Meghan's voice is all like, *duh*.

Artie groans. "Mad boring!"

"Cooking shows are huge!" Meghan snaps. "You just show everyone how you mix it up."

"Then wait half an hour?" Artie interrupts.

"No — then just pull out some that you've already baked, to show how they'll look." Meghan's eyes are huge. "Seriously, don't you people watch the Food Network?"

"I think that could work," I say.

"You would," Artie snaps, which sounds like an insult, but I can't really figure out if it is or not. She places the green wig neatly on the foam head where it lives. "Let's hold auditions."

I can't help feeling like Artie's trying to get me out of the show. Which I don't really mind. But Meghan isn't having it.

"It's a talent show, not a contest, Artie."

"I just don't want it to be lame!" Artie protests. "I don't want it to seem like we're a bunch of dorky five-year-olds putting on a puppet show behind the couch! Am I crazy?" She turns to me, but I'm lost in a memory of the two of us at age five, putting on a puppet show behind my couch. We used my Barbies to stage an original musical called *The Lonely Princess*. I thought it was pretty good. You know, considering we were five.

"The point is to have fun," Meghan says. "You *do* know how to do that, right, Artie?"

Artie sucks in a breath, and her face looks like she's about to go kablooie.

"Look, look, the talent show is supposed to be open to anyone who has a talent, and we just don't have time for auditions," I say quickly. "So it doesn't really —"

"Okay, if you want this to be a mess, that's fine." Artie pulls down another wig and starts yanking at the curls as if she wants to teach them a lesson.

I fiddle with the fringe at the end of my cape, feeling like I'm grasping at straws. "I think the trick is not to take this so seriously."

"If we're not going to take it seriously, then I don't want to do it at all," Artie replies. Her eyes are flat, her expression so cold that I'm tempted to wrap the cape around myself. "I'll perform in the show, but I don't want to help with it. Don't put my name on the program."

"We're having programs?" I ask just as Ms. Lang walks into the costume shop to check on us.

Artie gives her a smile, but Ms. Lang twists her mouth into a pucker-faced frown. "Well, Artemis, I think it's interesting that you're already backing out of the talent show. Did you forget that it's for a good cause?"

"We were just having a disagreement," Artie says. "I mean, I'll still be in the show. . . ."

"Most shows don't need more people to star in them." Ms. Lang's voice comes down hard like a heavy object. "They need people to make them happen."

"Of course, you're r-right . . ." Artie stammers. "I wasn't thinking —"

"I'm disappointed in you, Artemis, to be honest," Ms. Lang continues, as if Artie hasn't said anything. "I thought you understood the performing arts. I guess you still have a lot to learn. Anyway! You three are dismissed. I must say you've done a nice job here, surprisingly."

I finish stitching up the cape as Artie silently packs her book bag. She leaves in a hurry, red-faced and silent. Meghan puts away her ridiculous hat and claps a hand on my shoulder. "See you, Ms. Lang!" Meghan crows over her shoulder as we walk out the door.

The drama teacher nods, but she is still looking around.

"We don't need Artie's help, anyway," Meghan tells me.

"She made a good poster," I point out.

Meghan sighs heavily as she looks down the hall. Artie has already disappeared. "Artie's smart and she's organized. She's talented, too. But she's not a lot of fun."

"She used to be," I say, thinking of the puppet show.

Meghan looks up at the ceiling, as if she's thinking about this. "I can see it," she says finally, as if it's taking her a lot of effort to visualize Artie having fun.

I remember when I could, too.

Peppermint-Patty Cupcakes

(makes approximately 12 cupcakes)

I love peppermint. It always wakes me right up!
And when it's mixed with chocolate . . . yum!

INGREDIENTS:

    1/2 cup milk

    1/2 teaspoon apple cider vinegar

    1 cup all-purpose flour

    1/2 teaspoon baking powder

    3/4 teaspoon baking soda

    1/3 cup cocoa powder

    1/4 teaspoon salt

    1/2 cup semisweet chocolate chips

    1/4 cup yogurt

    3/4 cup granulated sugar

    1 teaspoon vanilla extract

    1 teaspoon peppermint extract

    1/3 cup canola oil

INSTRUCTIONS:

1. Preheat the oven to 350°F. Line a muffin pan with cupcake liners.

2. In a large bowl, whisk together the milk and vinegar, and set aside for a few minutes to curdle.

3. Sift the flour, baking powder, baking soda, cocoa powder, and salt into a large bowl, and mix together.

4. In a double boiler, melt the chocolate chips until smooth, then remove and cool to room temperature. If you prefer, you can instead melt the chocolate chips in a small bowl in the microwave, heating it on high for a few seconds at a time, then stirring until smooth. (Repeat heating if necessary, but don't overdo it!)

5. Once the milk has curdled, add in the yogurt, sugar, vanilla extract, peppermint extract, and oil, and stir together. Then add the melted chocolate and stir some more. With a whisk or handheld mixer, add the dry ingredients to the wet ones a little bit at a time and mix until no

lumps remain, stopping to scrape the sides of the bowl a few times.

6. Fill cupcake liners two-thirds of the way and bake for 18–22 minutes. Transfer to a cooling rack, and let cool completely before frosting.

7. With your (clean!) thumb, poke large holes into the center of each cupcake. Alternately, take a small knife and carve out a cone from the center of each cupcake to create a well. (You can discard the cones, or eat them.)

8. Fill a pastry bag with the peppermint frosting. (You can also make your own pastry bag by cutting off a corner from a plastic Ziploc bag.) Insert the tip of the pastry bag into each cupcake, and squeeze it to fill the cavity you created. Then swirl the frosting on top of the cupcake to cover the opening.

Peppermint Frosting

INGREDIENTS:

- 1 cup margarine or butter
- 3-1/2 cups confectioners' sugar
- 1-1/2 teaspoons peppermint extract
- 1–2 tablespoons milk

INSTRUCTIONS:

1. In a large bowl, with an electric mixer, cream the margarine or butter until it's a lighter color, about 2–3 minutes.

2. Slowly beat in the confectioners' sugar in 1/2-cup batches, adding a little bit of milk whenever the frosting becomes too thick. Add the peppermint extract and continue mixing on high speed for about 3–7 minutes, until the frosting is light and fluffy.

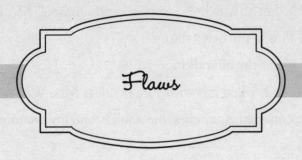

Flaws

"Is it Thursday already?" I tease as I walk into the café. Mr. Malik's usual Thursday bouquet is already installed by the cash register, and he and Gran are chatting over tea at one of the small tables near the front.

"I pride myself on my constancy," Mr. Malik says, and he smiles over the rim of his teacup.

"A most overlooked virtue," Gran agrees. "Especially these days. It's as if everyone has Attention Deficit Disorder."

"Gran!" I say.

"Well, everyone's checking their little devices and tapping away with their thumbs," Gran says with a sniff. She frowns at a nearby girl with a lip ring, who is texting madly.

"Ah, but this is how people communicate," Mr. Malik says. "This is the new talking."

"I prefer the old talking."

"As do I, when it is with you, my dear Mrs. Wilson." Mr. Malik's mustache twitches into a smile, and my grandmother laughs.

Mom is behind the counter as I tuck my book bag into a small cupboard and then go to wash my hands. When I get back, Marco is sitting on a stool, eating the last peppermint-patty cupcake.

"Hey!" I feel unreasonably happy to see him.

Marco smiles, but he can't talk because he's chewing.

"Hayley, sweetheart, I don't know if you were planning to make more cupcakes," Mom begins, and I hold up a hand.

"On it," I tell her.

She breathes a sigh of relief. "Good. Okay with you if I go check our supplies in the back? The monthly order is due today."

"Sure, Mom. I'm here. And Gran's right there, if I need help." I nod over at Gran and Mr. Malik's table, where they are laughing heartily, probably over some obscure literary reference.

Mom heads toward the back, and I pull out the mixing bowls and sugar, flour, butter, and cocoa.

"Refill on the chocolate cupcakes?" Marco asks as he pulls out his video camera.

"They ain't gonna bake themselves," I reply. "Marco, you aren't going to put this up on YouTube or something, are you?"

"Why — are you scared I'll reveal your secret ingredients?" Marco asks, breaking off another piece of cupcake and popping it into his mouth. He doesn't stop filming, though. "So how's the talent show going?" he asks.

"What's this about a talent show?" Mr. Malik asks, tuning in from his table.

"Hayley and her good friend are organizing the whole event," Gran boasts. She really seems proud. It's so cute.

Mr. Malik is, of course, the perfect audience for her bragging. He looks genuinely impressed. "Organizing the whole thing?" he repeats. "That's a big project! And will you be in the show?"

I laugh a little. "I don't have any talents."

"Cupcakes are your talent," Marco says.

I measure out the flour. "Well," I say as I sift it into a bowl, "Artie doesn't think it's a good idea."

"So what?" Marco demands.

"So — I don't want to embarrass Artie." I realize as I say this that I'm still hoping she'll help us with the show. She's the one who knows the most about theater, after all.

"I'm not getting this. Cupcakes are your life." Marco smashes a few chocolate crumbs with his finger and then pops them into his mouth.

"Yeah . . . but performing isn't my life." The mixer makes a low bumblebee hum as I cream the sugar and butter. "And it *is* Artie's life. I don't want to screw it up for her."

"Why not?"

"Because she's my friend, Marco!" My voice is louder than I intended, but Marco just nods. He turns off the camera. "I didn't mean to hurt your feelings," I say.

"You didn't," Marco replies. He pushes away his empty plate. "I've got to go. I'm meeting Tanisha."

"Another movie?" It makes me a little sick to ask.

"Math homework," Marco explains. "See you."

Well, that was short. Still, it was better than nothing. I work on the cupcakes a little longer, mixing in the flour and cocoa, then adding spices. I fill the cupcake liners and slide everything into the oven.

I'm wiping down the counter when Mr. Malik says good-bye, and Gran comes to join me. "What a pleasant afternoon," she says with a soft sigh.

The bell over the door jingles as Mr. Malik makes his way out into the cold winter air, back to his flower shop.

"But you don't look happy, my dear," Gran says. She peers at me closely, as if she can see through my skin, right down deep into the center of me.

"It's hard to be around Artie sometimes," I confess.

"Ah, Artie." Gran frowns.

"I thought we were becoming friends again, but . . ." I shake my head. "Ever since she stabbed me in the back, I don't know what to think."

Gran nods. "Well, sometimes you just need to . . . reevaluate."

"What?"

"Artie used to be your best friend. Then, for a while, she was your enemy." Gran wipes away some coffee grounds, thoughtful. "Perhaps she isn't quite either."

"What is she, then? My frenemy?"

"I have no idea what that means," Gran says. "I think she's just your friend . . . with flaws."

"Yeah." I think about that. I think of Marco, who once used me to cheat on a test. I think about Meghan, who has a bossy streak a mile wide. "They kind of all have flaws."

Gran reaches out and pulls me into a hug. She smells of cinnamon and vanilla. Like my Reassurance Cupcakes. "We all do," she whispers into my hair. "The trick is learning to live with them."

"The friends?" I ask. "Or the flaws?"

"Oh, whichever," Gran says. The timer rings, and I have to pull away to rescue my cupcakes from the oven. "Those look lovely."

"Thanks."

"Perhaps you should take one to Uzma," Gran suggests.

"What made you think of that?"

Gran chuckles. "Oh . . . friends with flaws, I suppose."

I breathe in the thick scent of pistachio and rosewater. Friends with flaws? Hmm. Maybe I *should* give one of these to Uzma. An Acceptance Cupcake.

Maybe I should give one to Artie, too.

"Ah, good, you're both here," Mom says as she returns from the back room. Gran loosens her hug, but still keeps one arm wrapped around my shoulders. "Mother, Denise just called."

"How's California?"

"Great. She's editing a trailer for the new Clooney movie. But she wants to come for a visit."

Yes, just in case you missed it: That's George Clooney. My aunt is a film editor. She does trailers, which means she gets to watch all kinds of cool movies before everyone else does. Denise lives in a gorgeous house and has the world's cutest pug, General Tzo, and basically has the best life on earth. Also, she is crazy cool and I love her. "When?"

"Next week," Mom announces. "She's got a little break coming up and was wondering if it would be convenient."

"Convenient?" Gran repeats. "It would be delightful!"

"That's what I said," Mom says. "She said she'd get a hotel, but I told her we could share a room."

"Even more delightful!" Gran is beaming.

"I can't wait!" I do a little dance behind the counter, which is totally not the kind of thing I normally do. But this is the best news I've had all week.

"She'll be here for the talent show," Mom says, which makes me so excited that I let out a little squeal. "I was thinking that maybe we'd have a little dinner party while she's here. We can invite some friends. Mr. Malik and Uzma?"

"Certainly. That sounds wonderful," Gran says, which is nice of her. I mean, do we really want to include Uzma? Probably not. But that would be rude.

"Maybe Ramon," Mom adds.

"By all means," Gran agrees.

Mom looks at me. "Sure," I say. I don't really want to share my aunt with anyone, but if Mr. Malik and Uzma are coming, I guess I don't really mind. Besides, it was nice to see Ramon for dinner last weekend, and I'm sure Denise will like him. "Chloe will probably want to ask Rupert," I suggest.

"Great idea," Mom says. "Do you want to invite anyone, Hayley?"

I consider inviting Meghan but decide she'd probably take over the entire conversation. Besides, I have a better idea. "How about Marco?"

"Fantastic," Mom says. "Okay██ ██ ██ ████ ████████
days might work for Mr. Malik." A██ ███ ███ ████ ██ ████
into the cold, toward the flower shop.

"Oh, how exciting," Gran says. "I'll ha████ ██ ████ ████
beef — Denise's favorite."

"Denise has been a vegetarian for three years.

"Oh, nonsense." Gran waves a careless hand at me. "She's
never a vegetarian around my roast beef."

I'm too excited to argue. I want to call Marco but remember that I'll have to wait until later. He's studying with
Tanisha right now.

I look down at the counter and realize that Mom left her
cell phone. She never even took it into the back room.

That's weird, I think. *Didn't she say that Denise just
called?*

So — wait. Why would she lie?

I think about the big dinner party, everyone inviting a
special friend.

I think about Denise coming into town suddenly.

I think about Ramon.

Then I think about this: *I have a wedding to plan.*

...gh the window, I see Mom hurrying through the ...stery darkness, on her way back from inviting Mr. Malik and his sister to dinner. Mom is smiling. She looks brilliant, like someone has just plugged her in.

I feel a little ill.

This doesn't mean anything, I tell myself. *Stop being paranoid.*

But it's not that easy, is it?

Confession:
I Found Something

A few days ago, I was in my mom's room, looking for her red necklace. She lets me borrow it sometimes, and I was wearing a black shirt that I thought it would look great with. Anyway, you're not really interested in the fashion recap, are you?

So I was in her room, looking through the rack of necklaces that she keeps on her bureau. I found the red one and was walking out the door when I spotted a magazine on Mom's nightstand. *Contemporary Bride.* A Post-it note was stuck in it, and I couldn't resist taking a look. I thought maybe she had marked a cool wedding cake, or fancy cupcakes, or something. But no. It was an article called, "Second Time Around: Tips for the Older Bride."

I felt like I'd just broken through ice on a frozen pond, shivery and desperate. Tips for the older bride? Why is Mom reading about that?

Because she has a wedding to plan, my brain whispered.

I closed the magazine and placed it back in its exact place.

How can Mom be marrying Ramon? She hardly even knows him! She's not really acting like someone who's crazy in love . . . not that I have any idea how someone who's crazy in love acts. I mean, in movies they're always buying flowers and running through the streets and stuff. Holding boom boxes over their heads in the rain. Mom has just been acting like . . . Mom.

It just feels so out of the blue. Like maybe my mom has this whole secret life that I don't know about. Which I guess she does. I didn't see the divorce coming, either.

I guess these huge, life-changing things can happen with absolutely no warning at all.

From the Phone Files

"Hey, Dad."

"Hayley! How are you? Ready to play some laser tag this Saturday?"

"Oh, right, I forgot we were doing that. Sure."

"Well, it was Chloe's turn to choose."

"No — sorry. I mean, it'll be fun."

"You okay? You sound distracted."

"Just . . . a lot of schoolwork and stuff."

"Sure. It can get overwhelming."

"Yeah."

"Well. Um, how's everything else going, Hayley? Anything else new?"

"Oh, I'm — planning a talent show with Meghan."

"That's great! Are you going to be in it?"

"Just the genius behind the curtain."

"Wow! I'm impressed."

"We haven't pulled it off yet."

"I'm impressed that you're trying."

"Thanks."

"So, when is this talent show?"

"Friday night. But, Dad, Aunt Denise is coming into town, and I think, um . . ."

"I completely understand. I'll see you Saturday. Do you want to put your sister on the phone?"

"Okay."

"Bye, Hayley."

"Dad?"

"Yeah, sweetie?"

"Would you tell me if you were going to get married again?"

"What?"

"Like, would you warn me —"

"I'm not getting married anytime soon."

"Okay, but . . ."

"Hayley, I would never, ever propose without telling you first."

"Really?"

"No way."

"I'd know?"

"You'd know. It would affect you, too."

"Thanks, Dad. I'll get Chloe now."

"Love you, Hayleycakes."

"Love you, too, Dad."

Pistachio-Rosewater Cupcakes

(makes approximately 12 cupcakes)

Sometimes, flavors that don't really seem like they'll go together make a good match. Be brave!

INGREDIENTS:

- 2/3 cup milk
- 1/2 cup vanilla yogurt
- 1/3 cup canola oil
- 3/4 cup plus 2 tablespoons granulated sugar
- 1–2 tablespoons rosewater
- 1 cup plus 2 tablespoons all-purpose flour
- 1/2 teaspoon baking powder
- 1/2 teaspoon baking soda
- 1/3 cup pistachio meal (finely ground toasted pistachios)
- 1/4 teaspoon salt
- 1/3 cup chopped pistachio nuts

INSTRUCTIONS:

1. Preheat the oven to 350°F. Line a muffin pan with cupcake liners.
2. In a large bowl, whisk together the milk, yogurt, oil, sugar, and rosewater, and set aside.
3. In a separate bowl, sift the flour, baking powder, baking soda, pistachio meal, and salt.
4. Slowly add the dry ingredients to the wet ones a little bit at a time, and combine using a whisk or handheld mixer until no lumps remain. Fold in the chopped pistachios.
5. Fill cupcake liners two-thirds of the way and bake for 20–22 minutes. Transfer to a cooling rack, and let cool completely before frosting.

Rosewater Frosting

INGREDIENTS:

    1 cup margarine or butter

    3-1/2 cups confectioners' sugar

    1 teaspoon rosewater

    1–2 tablespoons milk

INSTRUCTIONS:

1. In a large bowl, with an electric mixer, cream the margarine or butter until it's a lighter color, about 2–3 minutes.

2. Slowly beat in the confectioners' sugar in 1/2-cup batches, adding a little bit of milk whenever the frosting becomes too thick. Add the rosewater and continue mixing on high speed for about 3–7 minutes, until the frosting is light and fluffy.

3. OPTIONAL: Make the frosting a rosy shade of pink by adding a couple drops of red food coloring along with the rosewater.

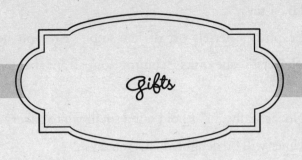

Gifts

"Hello?" I call as I step into Mr. Malik's shop. It's a lovely little place. A heavy, dark oak table sits at the center of the main room, covered in buckets of holly, feathery ferns, and elegant ivy topiaries. Wreaths of dried flowers cover the walls, and the refrigerated glass cases are packed with colorful arrangements. The whole place smells wonderful, the way you dream roses do, though they never quite live up to it. Soothing piano music plays in the background.

Uzma is behind the cash register, peering through a pair of reading glasses at a pile of receipts. Her lower lip is raised, and she reminds me of Mrs. McTibble's dog, whose tongue is always sticking out just a bit. Her eyebrows go up and she pulls off her glasses when she sees me. "Hayley, hello."

"Hi," I say.

She pushes herself off of her stool. "Are you here to buy flowers?" she asks, coming out from behind the counter.

"No, actually . . ." I hold out a small white bakery box.

"Umer will be delighted," Uzma says.

"Oh, no — it's for you," I explain.

"For me?" Uzma looks down at the box. Her eyes water up as she opens the box. "How thoughtful," she says. Her voice is quiet.

"I hope you like it," I add, just to cover up the awkwardness that has settled over the room.

"Is there someone on this planet who doesn't like cupcakes? Your grandmother put you up to this, I'll wager," Uzma says.

I just smile.

"Well!" Uzma says brightly. "I have something for you, too." She bustles behind the counter, her *salwar kameez* and shawl rustling. She pulls out a small white bag and spills the contents onto the counter. Five gold and teal bracelets clatter onto the dark wood.

"For me?"

"These are glass bangles," Uzma says, waving her hand dismissively, as if the bracelets aren't completely gorgeous. "Very traditional in Pakistan."

"They're awesome." I slide the bangles onto my wrist.

"I have some purple ones for Chloe, too," Uzma says, holding out another small bag. "You don't mind giving them to her, do you?"

"Of course not."

"She's seemed a little . . ." Uzma bounces her head a bit from side to side, like a bobblehead doll.

"Sad?"

"Yes."

I touch a soft yellow rose in a vase by the register, and my bracelets clink. "Rupert is moving away." I explain the situation with Rupert's father, and how there isn't anyone to take him to school in the morning, or home in the afternoon.

"And so — this friendship will end because of the school bus?" Uzma asks.

"Kind of."

"How unfortunate." Her mind seems faraway as her fingers flip open the lid of the small white bakery box. She takes a bite of the cupcake. "Ah . . . Well, cupcakes certainly do give one hope for better days, don't they?"

"I guess so," I say.

"I don't think we should allow this Rupert situation to go unresolved, do you?" Uzma asks.

"What do you mean?"

Uzma peels back the cupcake wrapper and takes another bite. "I think I'll have a word with Rupert's family."

"His foster family? Or his dad?"

"Everyone, I think," Uzma says.

I want to tell her that it isn't a good idea. But I have this feeling about Mr. Malik's sister: I don't think she's the kind of person you argue with.

She's more the kind of person you get out of the way of.

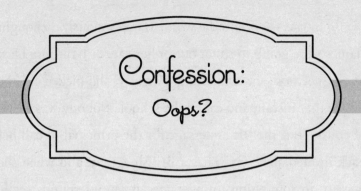

Confession:
Oops?

In second grade, I saw Charlie Oxwood draw red Xs on Ms. Jessup's glasses. She had left them on her desk, and when she left the room for a moment, Charlie went up, grabbed a marker, and drew on them.

Anyway, when Ms. Jessup came back and found her glasses, she was furious. She demanded to know who had drawn on her glasses. Of course, nobody in the class spoke up. Nobody wants to be a tattletale. Besides, Charlie was a creep. He would shoot spitballs at people and shove the kindergartners around. Nobody wanted to be on his bad side.

Well, that night, Gran came over for dinner. I was helping her make a pie in the kitchen, and when she asked me about school, I told her all about it.

Gran was — what's the word? Irate? Seriously, I thought flames were going to shoot out of her ears or lightning blast out of her nose, or something. Anyway, she picked up the phone that instant and called the school. Nobody was there, of course, but she left a message for the principal to call her back immediately. Gran has a British accent, and when she says to do something immediately, it always sounds really important.

"Will you tell them that I told you?" I asked Gran once she had hung up.

"I think they might be wise enough to make the connection without my help," Gran replied.

I must have looked kind of terrified, because Gran added, "I'll call Artemis's parents, as well, and have them confirm the story with her. And Marco's. All right? If several parents call the school with the same information, they'll have to do something. But no one will have to know that it was you who told."

Well, I wasn't sure I believed her . . . but everything happened just like she said it would. Charlie was given an in-school suspension for three days, and he never found out who told. And he was kind of a little bit less of a creep after that. I think that hearing that several of his classmates had turned him in made him more careful.

Oh, and Charlie's parents had to pay to have Ms. Jessup's glasses fixed. But that wasn't a big deal, because everyone knows the Oxwoods have way more money than brains.

I eventually told Marco and Artie the truth, and I always said that I'd told Gran accidentally — that I hadn't realized she would flip out the way she did. But sometimes I think maybe I did know. Maybe I wanted Charlie to get in trouble . . . but I didn't know how to handle it myself.

And the more I think about what just happened with Uzma, the more I think that maybe it wasn't exactly an accident. I want someone to talk to Rupert's family, but I can't do it. I don't even know them. Besides, I'm just a middle-school kid.

So — oops? I hope Uzma doesn't flip out all over Rupert's family.

Or that she flips out just enough to let him stay in Chloe's school.

Take a Flyer

"Why are you in the girls' room?" I ask as the door sighs shut behind me on Monday morning.

"Because I'm putting talent show flyers *everywhere*!" Meghan cries. "Look, do you like the glitter I added? I'm papering this school!"

"Yeah, they're great. But actually, I was asking Marco."

"Just capturing the magic on film." He's holding out his digital video camera, and Meghan turns to it with a grin and a thumbs-up.

"You know you can't be in here, right?" I ask. Maybe it's just because I don't have a brother, but I really don't want Marco to hear me pee.

Marco turns off the video camera. "Okay. I was done, anyway."

"We've got a ton of great acts, Hayley," Meghan gushes. "This is going to be amazing. And Mr. Lao said that he'd help run the lights — did I tell you that?"

"No. That's great."

"I can't believe the performance is Friday!" Meghan does a crazy little jig.

"Dang, I missed that." Marco frowns at his video camera. "That would've been an awesome shot."

"Why are you filming Meg putting up flyers, anyway?"

Marco shoves the camera into his backpack. "I just thought it would be fun to shoot everyone getting ready for the talent show. I got Kyle on piano, and David Lesser's dog act. I got the juggler."

"Did you get Artie?" I ask. Meghan shoots me a glare, but I ignore it.

"Not yet," Marco admits.

"You should submit the video as part of the show," I tell Marco, and Meghan does more crazy jigging.

"Brilliant! Brilliant! I've been looking for the perfect thing to close the show with!"

Marco whips out the camera again as Meghan twirls down the line of sinks. She's wearing blue tights and an orange wool A-line dress that swirls around her legs as she dances.

"Okay, well, I guess I have to put it in the show *now*," Marco says.

"Or you could submit it as evidence at Meghan's next sanity hearing," I joke.

Meghan ignores my comment and hands me a stack of flyers. "Would you help me put these up during lunch?" she asks.

"Sure."

"I'll help, too," Marco volunteers, and Meghan takes half of my stack and gives it to him. Just then, the bell rings. "See you later," Marco says.

"I'm getting so excited!" Meghan crows. "Artie is going to be so sorry that she blew us off!"

A toilet flushes and a stall door opens partway. A sixth grader pokes her head out of the stall. "Is he gone?"

"Sorry!" I say.

"Oh, wow — sorry." Meghan hands the sixth grader a flyer. "Here, come to the show."

The sixth grader glares and goes to wash her hands. She takes the flyer, though.

I guess that's the most important thing.

"Can I see?" I ask, leaning toward the stage curtain. The week has whizzed by, and it's finally the night of the talent show.

"It's bad luck," Artie snaps, gently pushing me away. She looks gorgeous. Her long auburn hair is up in a bun, and she's wearing a white sequined dress.

"You look like you're going to the Grammys," I tell her.

She blushes. "Thanks." I catch her sneaking a look toward the wings, where the dramaramas are warming up.

"Ooh! It's packed!" Meghan says as she peeks at the gap between the curtain and the stage. "Five minutes to showtime!"

Artie rolls her eyes. "It's bad luck to look at the audience before the show."

"I'm not performing," Meghan says.

"Me, either," I realize, so I go ahead and take a look while Artie huffs out a frustrated sigh. Meghan wasn't kidding — I don't think there's an open seat in the entire auditorium. I spot Gran, Mom, Chloe, and Aunt Denise in the third row.

They must have gotten here early. Dad and Aunt Denise haven't exactly been on the best terms since the divorce, so we agreed it would be better for him to sit this one out. Butterflies float in my stomach and I realize why Artie thinks it's bad luck to look at the audience before a show — it makes you nervous.

"Okay, everyone, we've got five minutes to curtain," Meghan repeats. She's holding a clipboard, which makes her look very official. And she's wearing a purple dress, which makes her look a bit like an eggplant. "Artemis, you're on third, okay? I've got to get David Lesser. . . ." And she scurries off to find David and his Corgi.

Artie sucks in her breath and puts her hands over her eyes.

"Are you okay?" I ask.

"Just nervous. I'll probably drop the microphone."

"You'll be fine." I give her this awkward little pat on the shoulder, and she gives me a half smile. And then I say, "You have a great voice, Artie. You're amazing." I don't know why I said that . . . except that it's the truth.

"Thanks," Artie says, and I have to fight the urge to say that I really, really mean it. She knows I mean it. I've told her lots of times before. "It's just that this is my chance . . ." She shrugs and doesn't finish the thought.

"To change Ms. Lang's mind about you?" I guess.

Artie looks at me, but she doesn't say anything. Just then, the audience goes quiet, and I realize that the lights have dimmed. Another moment, and the curtain goes up. David Lesser runs onto the stage with a Corgi in a tutu right behind him.

And we're on.

The Corgi act is seriously one of the cutest things I've ever seen, and the juggling act is pretty good, too. As it's finishing, I turn to Artie, who looks a little ill. "Break a leg," I say.

The panic doesn't budge from her face. "That's for actors."

"Well, break a vocal chord, then."

She looks at me and actually smiles. Then the audience applauds and Maria darts off and Artie walks out onto the stage. She stands at the center, and Mr. Lao puts a spotlight on her. Then Marco starts the CD. There are a few strains of violin music, and then Artie starts to sing.

She really does have a gorgeous voice. It's sweet and high, and surprisingly strong — it reaches out over the audience and fills the whole auditorium. It's a sad song, about a sailor who has left his love behind.

The audience is so still, it's as if everyone has forgotten to breathe.

"Amazing," Marco whispers in my ear. He has stepped away from the sound system.

Artie closes her eyes and lifts her voice into a high note —

And at that moment, a super bass beat bounces through the speakers.

"What's that?" Meghan asks. Her body is tensed, like she might just jump out at someone.

"Whazzup, Adams Middle School!" Jamil shouts as he bounces onto the stage.

"What the —" Marco makes a grab for Omar, who dodges away and slides out over the hardwood on his knees. Artie scoots out of his way.

"We're primed to rhyme!" Omar shouts.

"Like Greenwich Mean Time we're down to the minute —"

"And we're in it to win it —"

People are starting to boo.

"Who do they think they are?" Meghan snarls as she darts past me. "Kanye West?" Snapping out of my trance, I scurry after her.

But I'm not needed. Meghan runs up to Jamil and whacks him on the head with her clipboard. "You won't ruin my show!" she shrieks. The crowd goes nuts — cheering and screaming.

Artie watches the entire thing, white-faced and shell-shocked. Tears are spilling down her face. Omar tries to keep rapping, and all of a sudden, I'm filled with rage. There's a wastepaper basket by my foot. I grab it and dart onstage behind the chaos. Omar hasn't noticed me, which is how I manage to shove it over his head.

"That's not funny!" Jamil shouts as Meghan smacks him again. "Stop it!"

But it is funny. It's hilarious. The audience cracks up as Omar stumbles around with a trash can on his head, and Jamil is being attacked by a frenzied eggplant.

Thankfully, Marco manages to keep it together enough to think of lowering the curtain.

Once the curtain is down, we're in our own little world. The audience's laughter is muffled by the fabric.

"Get this off me!" Omar shouts, struggling with the trash can.

Meghan yanks it off his head. "Get out of here!" she shouts at him, then wheels on Jamil. "Both of you!"

Jamil throws up his arms, like he's trying to fend off a bear attack. "We were just trying —"

"You were trying to ruin the show!" Meghan screeches. "You were trying to make this whole thing about YOU! Well, it isn't about you! It's about everyone! So get out — GET OUT!"

I swear, I didn't realize those guys could run so fast.

I turn to Artie, who is as still as a stone. Tears flow down her face, and she doesn't even wipe them away. They collect beneath her chin. "Artie," I say gently, placing a hand on her shoulder. "Do you want to —" I was going to say, "start over," but Artie yanks away from me and runs — right off the stage, through the wings, and out the rear exit.

"This is a disaster," Meghan says. Her hair got messed up in the fight. She looks like a crazy Muppet. She puts a hand to her forehead. "What should I do?"

"Do?" Seriously, I can't believe Meghan is asking me this. "Go out there and announce the next act!"

"Really?"

"On with the show!" I say, pushing her toward the curtain.

Meghan nods, and takes a deep breath. "Okay," she says. "You're right. Would you let the dramaramas know they're up?"

"Get Marco to do it," I say as I rush toward the wings. "I've got to go find someone."

Meghan clenches her teeth. "Dead or alive," she says.

"Not those guys," I tell her. "Artie."

"Oh. I guess that makes more sense. Good luck." She gives me a quick hug, and the two of us hurry in opposite directions — Meghan toward the curtain, and me toward the rear exit.

The rear exit opens onto a courtyard. It's cold and clear, and the sky is stark black above me. The moon is a round, cool pebble high in the sky. A thin layer of snow crunches beneath my feet as I walk over to Artie, who is shivering and crying beside a pine tree.

"Artie." I give her an awkward little pat on the shoulder, and she surprises me by throwing her arms around my neck and pulling me into a hug.

"Did you see Chang and Devon? They were standing right there — right by the exit as I walked out. They didn't even" — she shudders, and her face twists — she's having trouble forcing out the words — "they didn't even . . . *look* at me."

I hadn't even noticed them there. "They're losers."

"But I love performing," Artie says. "And now . . . Ms. Lang will never let me into a show again. . . ."

For a moment, I don't know what to do. I rub her back a little. "It's okay," I tell her. Then, suddenly, a memory flashes into my mind. Very softly, because my voice is usually pretty uneven and croaky, I begin to sing a little song that Artie made up when we were small. "Don't be sad," I sing, "don't be sad . . . everything will be okay. . . ."

I expect Artie to laugh, but instead she pulls the hug tighter and whispers, "I'm so sorry."

"That wasn't your fault," I tell her. "Omar and Jamil would've interrupted anyone. They just love the attention."

Artie shakes her head, and her soft hair rubs against my neck. "Not that." Her tears are trickling onto my shoulder, freezing in the cold night air. I hear her swallow.

"Are you sorry that you didn't help out with the show?"

Artie sucks air deep into her lungs. "I'm sorry I've been such a bad friend."

My whole body feels limp, like a rag doll. I'm not cold anymore. I just feel like I'm suspended, floating over this whole scene. "Oh, Artie," I say.

"I've missed you so much," Artie says.

"I've missed you, too." I really mean it. I really miss the way we used to be — friends who knew everything about each other. And then, because I've never really understood it, I ask, "What . . . happened?"

Artie pulls away from me, wiping the tears from her face. She leaves her hands against her cheeks and looks up at me. It's dark, so I can't see well, but her eyes are wide as she looks at me. "Do you remember — what I told you about Marco?"

Artie had told me that she had a crush on him. "Yes."

"I saw him kiss you that day. . . . And I didn't know what to think."

"You *saw*?" I can't believe it.

"I can see your backyard from my bedroom, Hayley, remember?"

Now my hands fly to my cheeks. I feel them burning beneath my fingers. It had never, ever occurred to me. Never. "Oh my gosh . . . Artie, I —"

"I wanted to talk to you about it, but the next time I saw you, you told me that your parents were getting divorced," Artie said. "And I felt like an idiot for wanting to talk about Marco, so I didn't. But I didn't know what to say about your parents, either. . . ." Her tears are flowing again. I'm surprised to realize that my fingers are wet, too. "And I felt like a horrible friend, but I was also so angry and jealous. . . ." Her chin quivers and she shakes her head. "And then you moved away, and I couldn't go over to your house anymore when I wanted to escape from mine. . . . I didn't have anyone to talk to about Marco. I didn't have anyone to talk to about . . . you."

I wrap her in a hug again and hold her tight.

"It isn't easy to find a friend like you, Hayley," Artie says. Then she hiccups, which makes us both giggle.

"I know the feeling." But, of course, I've been luckier than Hayley. Meghan is a good friend. And things with Marco are different, but I haven't lost him completely.

We stand there in silence for a moment, until Artie hiccups again.

"I think we'd better go inside," I say.

"I'm freezing," Artie agrees.

So we go back to the exit door, holding hands.

Too bad it's locked.

Confession: I Never Thought of That

I never, ever thought of my parents' divorce as something that happened to anyone outside of my family. I knew it affected the two of them. I knew it affected me. I knew it affected Chloe.

But Artie?

I never thought about her.

I mean, okay, there are a lot of ways in which she was a bad friend to me when I needed her.

But I guess I wasn't so great, either.

I was so worried about the fact that we were growing apart that it never occurred to me to wonder if Artie was sad about it, too. I didn't even think about her at all.

Here's another funny thing: Artie's parents hardly ever even talk to each other. They never laugh. They're very efficient and intelligent, but they aren't *warm*.

And Marco's parents are strict and downright cold at times. Marco's mom always looks tired.

When Artie's and Marco's families would come over to our house, everyone got along fine — but I was always glad that I got the best parents. I never thought they would break up.

Artie's parents? Maybe. Marco's parents? Probably. But mine?

It just goes to show that no matter how well you know someone, or how much you love them, you never know what's going on in anyone's mind.

Everyone's just a living, breathing, walking mystery.

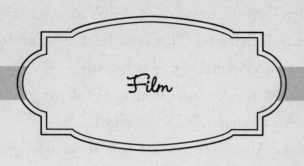

Film

Artie and I knock on the door, but nobody opens it. We don't want to bang on it, because the show is still going on, so we have to run around the building to get in the front door. This is actually kind of fun and it feels good to move, though the icy air is cold in my chest as I drink in deep gulps of air.

"Please let this be open," Artie says as she reaches for the door.

It swings open, and we blink in the surprising darkness of the auditorium. Onstage, a screen has been lowered, with a large image of Kyle seated at a piano. A moment later, he's talking to the camera. "I could play that piece blindfolded," he jokes, and the audience goes wild.

I realize we're watching Marco's mini documentary. I smile at how well Marco has captured Kyle's sense of humor as the scene switches, and suddenly I'm behind the counter at the Tea Room. I let out a little squeal as I watch myself mixing cupcake batter, and Artie elbows me in the ribs. Onscreen, Marco asks, "Will you be in the show?"

"Performing isn't my life," says the onscreen me. "And it *is* Artie's life. I don't want to screw it up for her."

I feel Artie's head swivel to look at me, but the documentary has cut to one of Artie's practice sessions. She's rehearsing in one of the schoolrooms, and her voice sounds just as good as it did earlier. Marco has managed to capture the dramatic moment when she really reaches out with an almost impossible high note — it's the part of the song that we missed, and it makes the hairs on the back of my neck stand up. And, suddenly, we're watching Meghan hang up posters in the bathroom. "Why are you working so hard for this show?" Marco asks.

"I just can't wait to see what everyone has planned!" Meghan says. She beams into the camera for a moment, and then — black.

THE END flashes onscreen in white letters. A FILM BY MARCO DE LUCA.

The audience goes nuts, screaming and cheering. And then, suddenly, someone starts to chant. At first, I can't make out the words. But I hear Artie suck in her breath, and then I realize that they're chanting, "We want Art-ie! We want Art-ie!"

"What should I do?" She looks shocked.

"Go up there!" I tell her, nudging her down the aisle. She takes a step, then looks over her shoulder at me. "Do it!"

So she walks forward, and as people realize she's coming toward the stage, the cheering gets louder and crazier until it's deafening. Artie climbs the side stairs, and when Meghan sees her, she comes dashing from the wings with a microphone. Mr. Lao raises the movie screen and puts the spotlight back on her. Artie takes a deep breath and closes her eyes as the audience settles down. Then her eyes snap open, and it's like there's a whole new Artie there. She almost doesn't need a spotlight — she's magnetic.

And then she starts to sing.

Her voice is huge. It's almost like a physical thing — a

rope you could catch in midair, or maybe a cloud that could lift you and carry you away. It's so beautiful that I feel my throat close. My breath is wheezy.

If Omar and Jamil appear, I think, *I will seriously go ballistic all over them.*

But they don't. Instead, the song reaches out and pulls me in and I want it to go on and on. But, of course, it can't, and suddenly, it's over.

The auditorium is silent, as if everyone needs to just breathe for a moment, and then the place explodes. People jump to their feet. Electricity shoots through the crowd. Artie looks shy and embarrassed, but she curtsies and everyone just keeps cheering. Finally, she waves and walks off, but the crowd keeps cheering.

Meghan leads everyone who was in the show out onto the stage for a bow, and the audience goes wild. I'm still standing in the aisle, and Meghan manages to spot me in the crowd. She gives me a grin and a thumbs-up.

I grin back.

Sometimes, the craziest ideas really *are* the best ones.

*   *   *

The scene backstage is nuts. Everyone is crying and hugging, or squealing and hugging, or high-fiving, or running around in circles and barking (that last one is just the Corgi).

Meghan grabs me and gives me a huge squeeze. "We did it!"

"It was a great show," I tell her, even though I only saw part of it.

Just then, Artie comes over. Her mascara is all smeary, but she's beaming. "I'm so glad you made me go up there!" she says.

"You were great," Meghan tells her, her voice warm.

"Thank you — so were you," Artie gushes, and I let out a little snort of surprise. Artie twirls the end of a lock of hair that has escaped her updo. "I don't know if I'll get another chance to perform anytime soon, though."

"Why not?" Meghan demands. "You were amazing. You should be performing every *week*!"

Artie rolls her eyes a little, but she's smiling. "Well, I don't think Ms. Lang was impressed."

Meghan sniffs. "What does she have to do with anything?"

"Meg's right," I agree. "You could put on your own show, couldn't you?"

Artie bites her lip. "I'd need Ms. Lang's permission."

"No," Meghan corrects her, "you'd need permission from someone in the drama department."

"How about Mr. Lao?" I suggest.

"Bingo," Meghan says.

Artie cocks her head and looks at Meghan in a way I've never seen her look at Meghan before. It's as if — for the first time ever — Artie can see why someone would think Meghan is cool. "That's a really good idea."

"Let's go say hi to him now," Meghan says, grabbing Artie's hand and dragging her off. Artie flashes me a panicked look over her shoulder, but I just give her a little wave.

"Good luck!" I call.

"Hayley?" someone says over my shoulder. When I turn, I see Kyle's smiling face. "You did a great job on the show."

"Oh, thanks. I didn't really do anything."

Kyle laughs. "Really? So — Meghan and Artie just really got along and enjoyed working together?"

"Well . . . not exactly."

"Right. That's your talent, Fred. You bring out the best in people."

I feel every hair on my head. I hear the blood rushing through my ears. I bring out the best in people? "I'm sorry I missed hearing you play the piano."

"You can hear that anytime," Kyle says.

I giggle like a moron, and the sound makes Kyle laugh. But not like he's laughing at me. More like he thinks I'm funny, or like I made him happy. I get this weird feeling — like someone's watching me. When I turn, I see Marco. He's standing off to the side, almost underneath the glowing red EXIT sign. He's holding the video camera to his eye. When I look at him, he lowers it and pushes the OFF button.

Marco was filming me talking to Kyle. My heart throbs in my chest as he looks down at the screen.

And once again, I wonder what he sees there.

Sweet

"That was fantastic!" Aunt Denise gushes once we're home. "I really loved Marco's film!" We're in Gran's tiny upstairs kitchen, and my aunt is helping me load a plate full of cupcakes. Raspberry flavor.

"Wasn't it great?" I agree.

Marco blushes. "Aw, come on."

"You've got talent, for sure," my aunt tells him.

Mom pops her head into the kitchen doorway. "How's it going in here?" she asks.

"Hayley's got everything covered," Aunt Denise assures her.

Mom takes a deep breath and lets it out slowly. I can hear Ramon telling a story at the table. A moment later, everyone laughs. So far, this dinner party has been super fun. Mr.

Malik and Ramon have been chatting away, and Aunt Denise — who has been seated beside Uzma — can talk to anyone. Chloe can't stop talking about the ballerina dog, and Rupert keeps repeating, "But how can you train it to *appreciate* the music?"

I was just starting to think that everything was going to be okay and I was just a paranoid nutburger when Mom did that slow breath thing.

"What's up?" I ask her as Marco takes the seat beside Rupert.

She looks over her shoulder and rakes her fingers through her hair. "Nothing. You ready?"

"Almost," Denise says. But she's smiling a little smile that doesn't look like it has anything to do with cupcakes.

"Why are you smiling?" I ask her.

Denise's eyebrows shoot up, and she looks over at Mom. My mother gives her head a quick little shake and says, "There's going to be an announcement, that's all."

"An announcement?" I repeat. My aunt is now smiling so broadly that her dimples are showing. It's funny to see a grown woman with dimples.

"Ready?" Mom urges.

"Sure," I say, and nobody but me seems to notice the quaver in my voice.

Denise actually starts humming as she picks up the platter of cupcakes. She gives me a wink, and now I'm sure, positive, certain that Something Big is happening. The lasagna we had for dinner is swimming around in my stomach, and so I try Mom's technique — I suck in a deep breath and let it out slowly. It doesn't help.

Don't start bawling when he asks, I tell myself. *Act like you're happy.*

It'sfineit'sfineit'sfineit'sfine, I repeat mentally, like a — what's it called? That yoga term? A mantra? I repeat it all the way into the dining room. Mr. Malik's wrinkles dance into a smile that uses his whole face. "Cupcakes by the master!" he says.

"Those are beautiful, Hayley," Ramon puts in.

"Amazing, as usual," Marco agrees.

Denise slides into her seat beside Uzma and grins at my mom.

Mom smiles back and takes in a shaky breath. "So — everyone — we, uh, I'm so glad that you all could join us here tonight. There's, um, something very special . . ."

I don't even realize I'm doing it, but I grab my sister's hand. She looks at me, curious, but she doesn't let go.

Mom has paused, almost expectantly. And then Mr. Malik stands up.

"Dear friends," he says. "Thank you so much for having my sister and me into your home."

I love Mr. Malik, but right now, I wish he would just sit down, so we can get this horrible "announcement" over with. I feel like a fish that has just flopped onto a riverbank — I can hardly breathe.

"You are all very, very dear to us," Mr. Malik says.

"Hear, hear," Gran says.

Mr. Malik smiles at her. "In the eighteen years that I have owned the flower shop beside your tea shop, Mrs. Wilson," Mr. Malik says, "we have grown close, and become the best of friends, have we not?"

"Indeed we have," Gran agrees.

"And we have spent many happy afternoons together, drinking tea and talking."

"Many afternoons." Gran's blue eyes twinkle.

"In the time that your daughter, Margaret, and her daughters, Chloe and Hayley, have come to live with you, it has been my great privilege and honor to get to know them, and to feel that they are almost my own dear family."

"Aww — we love you, too!" Chloe chirps.

Uzma murmurs her agreement. I look over at Mom, who is crying now, and I wonder if she's upset that Mr. Malik has ruined her announcement. I bite my lips to keep from screaming.

"And, Denise, I hope to get to know you better in the future," Mr. Malik goes on.

"You can count on it," my aunt tells him.

Mr. Malik smiles at her, then turns to Gran and takes her hand. She cocks her head in surprise, but she is still smiling. "And so, my dear Mrs. Wilson, as we have enjoyed so many happy afternoons together, and so many years, I feel it's quite natural that we should wish to do this as often as possible, for as many years as we can. In the words of our beloved Charles Dickens, 'Come, let's be a comfortable couple, and take care of each other! How glad we shall be, that we have somebody that we are fond of always, to talk to and sit with.'" And I'm still trying to figure out why Mr. Malik is gushing on and on about friendship when he kneels down on one knee, and Uzma starts blubbering into her napkin, and Gran's face lights up, and I realize that *this is the announcement*.

It doesn't have anything to do with Mom at all.

"Will you do me the honor of becoming my wife?" Mr. Malik asks.

"Oh my gosh!" Chloe cries.

"Oh, Mr. Malik, don't be absurd," Gran replies. "Of course I will."

Then Mr. Malik kisses Gran on the cheek, and everyone starts talking at once, and Chloe jumps out of her chair, and I do all I can not to fall out of mine, and Rupert shakes my hand gravely and congratulates me on my new grandfather. Marco runs for his video camera, Aunt Denise and Mom are hugging and crying, and Uzma can't stop blubbering as Ramon pats her on the back awkwardly, and it's just about the strangest, most stunning thing that has ever happened. Ever.

And finally everyone settles down, and Mom says, "How about those cupcakes!" and everyone agrees that it's a great idea. I notice that Gran has pulled her chair closer to Mr. Malik's, and they are both beaming and looking kind of excited and proud.

Mom starts handing out cupcakes, and Chloe says, "Oh, this is just so great. Now if only Rupert weren't moving away, everything would be perfect." She looks over at him sadly, but Rupert is grinning at Uzma, who clears her throat.

"Well, it seems that a solution to Rupert's schooling has been found," Uzma announces.

"What?" Chloe gasps.

"It's true!" Rupert crows. "Uzma's going to drive me!"

"What?" This time it's me who's shocked.

"I'm an early riser, anyway," Uzma says primly. "I'll simply pick up Rupert and take him to school. Then I'll bring him here afterward, and he can stay at the Tea Room until his father can pick him up."

Chloe screeches and wraps Rupert in a huge hug. For a moment, he doesn't seem to know what to do. Then he gives her an awkward hug back.

"Well, I think everyone agrees that it's terribly disruptive to change schools at this time of year," Uzma says, and I have no doubt that she's using the exact words she used with Rupert's dad and family. I shake my head. Uzma is not to be trifled with.

You've got to give her respect, or she'll roll right over you.

"This is the best day of my life!" Chloe cries. "I'll remember this forever!" She stands up and twirls around like a crazy spinning top, which makes everyone crack up.

I look over at Gran, who is smiling, but looks a little teary. Mr. Malik is beside her, and he's so happy that he looks like he might just float right up to the ceiling. Uzma looks pleased and proud. Rupert laughs at Chloe, but seems shy, as if he's not used to having this much attention.

I wonder what I look like. Maybe as if I've been hit on the head with something heavy. Not in pain, just — stunned.

Anyway, I know one thing for sure: Everyone around me is happy. The room is buzzing with it. And I'm happy, too.

Mom passes out the cupcakes, and I take a bite.

"Life is sweet," Mr. Malik says as he tastes his.

Yes. That's right. At this moment, life is sweet. And Chloe is right — none of us will ever, ever forget this night.

Peanut Butter and Jelly French Macarons

(makes approximately two dozen macarons)

It's important to try something new once in a while. Whenever I do that, I try to stick to flavors that I know will work well together. You don't want your flavors to end up in a fight!

INGREDIENTS:

- 1-1/2 cups confectioners' sugar
- 1/2 cup almond flour/meal
- 1/3 cup peanut flour/meal, or ground roasted peanuts, unsalted
- 3 large egg whites, at room temperature
- 5 tablespoons granulated sugar
- 1 teaspoon vanilla extract
- Parchment paper
- Pastry bag with a 0.4 inch tip

INSTRUCTIONS:

1. Cut two sheets of parchment paper to the size of your baking sheets. Draw 1-inch circles on the paper, spacing them at least a 1/2-inch apart. This will be your guide when squeezing out the macaron batter.

2. In a food processor, grind together the confectioners' sugar, almond flour, and peanut flour or ground roasted peanuts to a fine powder. Sift the mixture through a medium-mesh sieve and set aside.

3. In a stainless steel bowl, beat the egg whites on high speed until they are foamy. Slowly add the granulated sugar to the egg whites while still beating them with your mixer. After all the sugar has been added, add the vanilla extract and beat the egg whites on high speed until they reach stiff, glossy peaks. (Check by removing your mixer from the meringue to see if the peak left behind keeps its shape.)

4. Scrape the sides of the bowl so all the meringue is at the bottom. Add half of the sifted flour mixture to the meringue. Using a spatula fold it in by scooping it up from the bottom of the bowl. (Don't just "stir" like you would for cupcake batter, or you will destroy the meringue.) Add the rest of the flour and fully combine.

5. Learn a new term: *macaronnage*. When all the flour is combined, press and spread out the batter against the bowl's sides. Scoop the batter from the bottom and turn it upside down. Repeat this process of pressing/spreading, then scooping about 15 times.

   TIP: If the macaronnage step is repeated less than 10 times, the baked macarons lack luster. But repeat more than 20 times and oil stains may remain on the surface when the macarons are baked.

6. Learn another term: *macaronner*. When the batter becomes nicely firm and drips slowly as you scoop it with a spatula, the mixture is done.

7. Grab a large pastry bag with a tip that has about a 0.4 inch/1.01 centimeter circular opening. Twist the pastry bag to hold the tip tightly. This will prevent batter from leaking out while putting it inside the pastry bag.

8. Place the pastry bag, tip down, in a deep cup, and fold over the end of the bag to hold in place. Pour the batter in, then after it's all inside, twist the bag's end and clip it (or use a rubber band) to prevent batter from being squeezed out.

9. Take your parchment-lined baking sheets and slowly squeeze out circles of batter (oh yeah, you should untwist the pastry bag where the tip is), following your pattern. Be careful, since the batter tends to spread a little after being squeezed.

10. When the sheet is filled with batter, rap it firmly against the counter or other flat surface to help form the "foot" characteristic of French macarons.

11. Dry the batter at room temperature, uncovered, for 15–30 minutes. At this point, you can preheat your oven to 375°F, placing oven racks in the center of the oven.

12. The macarons are ready for baking when they form a slight crust, so test one with your finger — if it doesn't stick to your finger, the batter is ready.

13. Bake the macarons for 15–18 minutes, until slightly crisp. To bake evenly, make sure to rotate the tray halfway through baking. When done, remove from the oven and allow to cool completely before adding the filling.

Jam Buttercream Filling

INGREDIENTS:

    1/2 cup unsalted butter, room temperature

    Pinch of salt

    3/4 cup confectioners' sugar

    2 tablespoons jam (your choice in flavor — I love strawberry)

INSTRUCTIONS:

1. In a medium bowl, whip the butter and salt with a mixer until fluffy. Slowly add the confectioners' sugar and beat until completely combined.

2. Add the jam and continue beating until light and fluffy. Take the macarons you've made and create little sandwiches with the filling. Refrigerate macarons up to one week.

QUICK OPTION: just fill the macarons with plain jam, but these macarons will have to be consumed within one day!

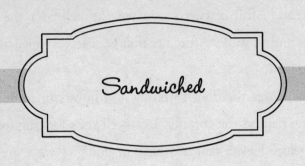

Sandwiched

"Oooh, little sandwich cookies!" Meghan says as I place a plate on the table in front of her. "So cute!"

"They're macarons," I explain. "French — and gluten free."

"Lucky me!" Meghan takes a bite of one. "So good! Are they easy to make?"

"Totally not."

"Okay, then I won't even ask for the recipe. I'll just come here."

I smile and take a bite of a peanut butter and jelly macaron. I messed up three batches before I finally managed to make one come out right. But these were perfect — light and crisp with a smooth, sweet center.

I'm just reaching for my thick china mug — which is

dangerously full of cocoa — when the bell over the door jingles and in walks Artie, her orange scarf wrapped almost to her eyes.

She closes the door carefully and hovers in front of it, looking behind the counter. I can tell she's looking for me, and before I even realize what I'm doing, I wave and say, "Over here!"

Artie unwinds her scarf, and her cheeks bloom pink in the warm café. "Hi," she says as she sits down at our table.

"Eat this," Meghan says, holding out a cookie.

Artie shakes her head. "Meghan, do you have to make everything sound so bossy?"

A flash of worry shoots through me, but Meghan doesn't snap. She just says, "I don't like to give people choices. Then they might say no."

Artie laughs and takes the cookie. "Mmm."

"Aren't you glad you listened to me?" Meghan asks.

Artie rolls her eyes. "I'm glad that Hayley made these cookies. How's that?"

"I'm branching out," I announce.

"But you'll still make cupcakes sometimes, right?" Artie asks. "I mean — I'd hate for those to disappear forever."

"Oh, I'll still make cupcakes," I promise. "In fact — I might have to make some for a special occasion soon." And I explain about Gran and Mr. Malik.

"Whoa." Meghan's eyes are wide. "Cool!"

"It's so romantic," Artie says.

"Yeah, it is, kind of," I agree.

Artie looks around the café and takes another thoughtful bite of her cookie. "Everything's changing."

"Everything is always changing," Meghan points out.

"True," Artie admits. "But it's a little hard."

"Hard?" Meghan looks shocked. "You mean exciting!"

"*She* means hard," I say, pointing at Artie. "*You* mean exciting. And you're both right."

"Hmm." Meghan nods. "Okay."

"Good point, Hayley," Artie says.

I take a sip of my cocoa, letting myself savor the warm sweetness. I don't know if Artie and Meghan will ever be best friends. I don't know if I'll ever be really close to Artie again, either. But at least we can get along.

And I'm glad to have them both.

Flaws and all.

Acknowledgments

I would like to gratefully acknowledge the help of my sister, Zoë Papademetriou, who created the recipes in this book. I would also like to thank my editor Anamika Bhatnagar for her insight and input, and my agent Rosemary Stimola for her unwavering enthusiasm. Huge thanks to Starr Mayo and Jackie Hornberger, whose help and high standards are essential to this series. As always, a loving hug to my husband and daughter. Thank you to Nerissa Nields for her support of my blog, and to Ellen Wittlinger, Nancy Werlin, Liza Ketchum, and Pat Collins for their willingness to share their work and careful attention to mine. And a huge shout-out to my fellow writers (and friends) at Vermont College of Fine Arts!

Don't miss Hayley's latest confessions!

Hayley's family's tea shop is abuzz with some great news: Gran's getting married! But Hayley's best friends are fighting like crazy, and every time she tries to make a wedding cake, it turns into a royal disaster. Everything seems to be falling into place for Gran, for Hayley's parents, and even for little sister Chloe — but will there be a happy ending for Hayley?

Candy Apple Books

Fresh. Fun. Sweet.
Take your pick!

More Sweet Reads from Lisa Papademetriou!

SCHOLASTIC

scholastic.com/candyapple

SCHOLASTIC and associated logos are trademarks
and/or registered trademarks of Scholastic Inc.

Available in print
and eBook editions

CANDYp